# Chilled to the Bone:
a Bardstown Halloween Anthology

For more information about the Bardstown Writers visit:

**www.bardstownwriters.btck.co.uk**

# Chilled to the Bone:
a Bardstown Halloween Anthology

**Bardstown Writers**

Bardstown Press

First published in 2015 by Bardstown Press

Copyright © Bardstown Press 2015
Individual contributors © the contributors, 2015

The right of the Bardstown Writers to be
identified as the authors of this work has been
asserted by them in accordance with the
Copyright, Designs and Patents Act 1988

*All characters and events in these pieces, other than those
clearly in the public domain, are fictitious and any
resemblance to real persons, living or dead is purely
coincidental.*

ISBN 978-0-9930096-2-4

Cover design by Grace Kemp

Bardstown Writers' logo designed by
Elliott Parkes

# Chilled to the Bone:
a Bardstown Halloween Anthology

# **CONTENTS**

| | |
|---|---:|
| The Silver Shoe | 1 |
| The Halloween Mask | 9 |
| Dance Macabre | 21 |
| The Lake at Foxcote | 25 |
| Old Pumpkin Head | 33 |
| Unwanted | 39 |
| Skin Treatment | 41 |
| Don't Open the Attachment! | 49 |
| Pull Me Close | 59 |
| Ghost Seeking | 65 |
| Treat or Trick? | 71 |
| No Party | 81 |
| The Offering | 87 |
| Face to Face | 97 |
| The Challenge | 107 |
| Diamorphine | 115 |
| For Better for Worse | 123 |
| | |
| About the Authors | 133 |
| Acknowledgements | 141 |

# The Silver Shoe

Tap, tap, tap, tap, tap. She was advancing very slowly towards his bed. Tap, tap, tap. He went rigid with fear. He screamed.

David slept in a truckle bed in the same room as his mother. A curtain decorated with a pattern of teddy bears and toy soldiers screened him from his mother's bed. He almost always ended the night with her unless his father was home on leave. In that freezing winter they kept each other warm. Facing their beds was a small chest of drawers. The top two drawers contained his mother's underwear and nightdresses, the bottom one a jumble of bits and pieces, lengths of elastic, knitting needles, a wooden mushroom for darning socks, a couple of half used candles, a tin box with letters from his father and a small silvery metal shoe. It was about two inches long, a woman's shoe, and through the lace holes was threaded a faded, blue velvet ribbon. He imagined it must have belonged to a very small woman a long time ago. She wouldn't have been more than twelve inches tall. He found that very creepy. He wondered why there was only one shoe and decided she must have had only one leg and walked with a crutch. The thought made him go cold. He imagined the tap, tap, tap of her little metal shoe across the lino. She would have had a shrill, squeaky voice. As he lay in bed at night he would hear her tapping her way towards his bed. His screams brought his mother but he could never bring himself to explain his terrors.

Downstairs his grandmother was knitting, as close to the fire as she could get.

'Another nightmare,' said his mother and picked up the book she had been reading. Her mother was a widow and she the only child. Her mother had lost her own husband in the first world war and never remarried. But she was prone to fits of depression and a fatalistic belief that her daughter's husband would be slaughtered like hers had been. Not that she'd loved him.

'He was a rat,' she used to say bitterly, 'and better dead.'

David eventually went to sleep and in the daylight he would dare himself to open the drawer and take out the shoe. It felt heavy in his hand and icy. He knew it was just waiting to be brought to life. He thought of Aladdin's lamp and felt a horrid compulsion to rub it. He hated to imagine what evil spirit might appear! Hastily he thrust it back out of sight.

Then one day his mother announced, 'Your Dad'll be coming home soon.'

David went back to his comic. He hardly knew his father and if he tried to recall what he looked like he could only evoke a scratchy battle dress and shiny black boots. His arrival meant a disruption to their lives that put them all on edge. His mother was especially keyed up. She suddenly became very fussy, pestering David about things that were often ignored, like elbows on the table at mealtimes, washing his hands before eating and cleaning his nails. She had her hair done; she bought a new lipstick. She became very nervy and it affected David. He thought his father must be someone to fear. Yet in his company she became playful, her face lit up with smiles and he often heard them laughing and giggling in bed. Moreover, his father brought him strange presents, like a set of Chinese chequers with counters made of small bullet cases. He once produced a huge bag of barley sugar which cascaded onto the kitchen table, a torrent of transparent golden nuggets wrapped in cellophane. They all gazed in wonder. David didn't even know what sweets were until then and he was convinced that, holding out his hands towards the glowing pile, his hands became warm, as though the sweets were hot embers.

Goodness knows, they all needed warmth. The winter continued relentlessly. Pipes froze; the outside loo became unusable and they had to resort to chamber pots. However many layers they wore the chill seemed to penetrate right to their bones. Even huddled around the fire their breath could be seen in faint white plumes. One night David felt shaky, his body leaden. He couldn't eat and was taken to bed with a hot water bottle. His mother left the landing light on and he fell asleep almost immediately. In the morning he couldn't get up. He didn't have the strength to combat the cold. He just wanted to stay in his warm cocoon under the blankets. His mother brought him a drink and an aspirin. He fell asleep again. When he next woke he was burning hot and he could feel the sweat trickling over his ribcage. His mind felt like a ball of string that had got tangled and knotted.

Not long after, his mother found him still sitting on the icy floor clutching the shoe, trance-like and shaking with fever. She put him back into bed still clutching the shoe and went to the telephone box to call the doctor.

It was then he heard the tap tap tapping across the floor. He thought he must be dying and the little old woman was coming to take him away. Was it the fever that made him indifferent? He didn't scream. He just waited for her tiny wizened face to appear above his bedclothes. The tapping intensified, speeded up, became staccato with a machine gun intensity. At the same time the sheet which he had pulled up to his nose was illuminated with sudden startling flashes as though lightning was playing on a distant landscape and an irregular percussive thunder deafened his ears. The bedclothes were a crushing weight preventing any movement. A face slowly appeared in front of him, not that of an old woman but of a young man. A face streaked with mud and blood, with horrified, staring eyes that looked into his. There was just the glimpse of a battledress and more blood. The man was speaking urgently against the booming and rattling. David strained to catch what he said. He was imploring, he was desperate; his face was twisted with pain and urgency.

'Tell her I love her,' was all David caught. The face continued mouthing, but the rest was drowned in the background roar. Before he could react the face fell back below the horizon of bedding and was lost. The silence when it came was as shattering as the noise had been.

When he woke his mother and the doctor were beside his bed. He heard her say, '..and he'll be here on leave in a couple of days.'

The vision he had witnessed instantly switched on in his mind. Now he realised what it meant. His mother would never see her husband again. And he knew he could never tell her that.

His fever remained worryingly high. He developed severe pain in his abdomen. The next day he was driven to the hospital for an emergency operation to have his appendix removed. 'Just in time,' said the surgeon but David remained very ill, and remembered nothing of the subsequent days.

One day he became aware of visitors. 'And how's our wounded hero?'

And there was his father, standing beside him holding his mother's hand, a self-conscious smile on his face. 'Look, I've brought you this.' He produced a green canvas bag. David slipped his hand inside and pulled out some marbles, not the ordinary sort but as big as golf balls with curly patterns inside. He tried to smile but he burst into tears instead.

Soon, his father would be demobbed. They would move back to London leaving his grandmother alone again in her country cottage. The little shoe was forgotten. Only decades later, when his mother died and he was looking through her old photos, did he realise with a shock that the apparition had been her father. He came across an old studio photo which must have been taken before 1914. His grandfather appeared dapper in a formal suit with a white flower in his buttonhole and a watch chain looped across his waistcoat. His hair was slicked back with a razor sharp parting.

He was looking straight at the camera with a self-satisfied air. His wife was looking up at him as though in admiration. And was that the silver shoe she was holding, just hidden by the small bouquet in her hand? He couldn't be sure. He would have liked to think it was a gift, a love token perhaps. He wondered what had become of the shoe. He had no recollection of it after his illness. He would like to have held it again, to see if it would evoke a nostalgic sense of his childhood. But he knew that his childhood, like the silver shoe and the words his grandfather had tried to convey, was beyond recall.

© Nick Sproxton 2015

Chilled to the Bone

# The Halloween Mask

A Mappleford Mysteries story for 8–12 year olds

Blood shot eyes glared back at Toby. Deep slashes cut across the cheeks and green pus oozed from the corners of the mouth. A smile slowly spread across the grey, wrinkled skin, revealing yellow teeth and an air of madness.

Toby stood in the doorway of his house, grinning. 'Brilliant zombie mask George. Very scary! Wait here. I'll grab my stuff.'

Toby picked up his bag from the hallway and checked his reflection in the mirror, making sure his bright red hair was sticking up over his vampire mask. He slammed the front door shut behind him and walked down the garden path, looking for his friend.

'George! Where are you?'

A hand grabbed Toby's shoulder and a plump skeleton jumped in front of him. 'Cool your boots Dracula! I'm here.'

George the skeleton stood with Pali and Olivia. Pali was wearing a werewolf mask and Olivia was dressed as a witch. The werewolf sneezed and the witch grabbed Toby by the arm, pulling him along the path.

'Come on. Let's go trick or treating before the village party starts.'

Toby looked over his shoulder as he was marched through the village. 'George, how did you get changed so quickly?'

George lowered his mask from his face and let it hang around his neck. He pulled his black and white skeleton t-shirt over his bulging belly. The material stretched to its limit and the bony rib cage distorted.

'Huh?'

'A second ago you were a zombie and now you're a skeleton.'

Before George could answer, Olivia knocked loudly on the vicarage door. 'Trick or treat!'

Mrs Bloomington, the vicar's wife, opened the door and oohed at the scary foursome facing her. 'Fantastic. Just like the real thing. Now, take a treat. George, put those three back...no need to be greedy.'

After grumbling his way around the village, George stopped to inspect his stash of sweets. 'Why is everyone being so tight? I've only got a few chews and a cupcake. Let's try our luck in the pub.'

Toby shook his vampire head. 'What if the Bradley twins are about?' The Bradley twins lived above the pub and had made Toby's life a misery ever since he had moved to the quiet village of Mappleford.

'Easy. I'll put a spell on them,' Olivia said, pushing Toby and Pali through the door.

George was about to follow when a heavy, bony hand clamped down on his shoulder. Before he could react, long, filthy fingernails plunged into his goodie bag and scooped out the cake. George swung around just in time to see a blur of scaly grey skin covered with green pus turn around and lope off.

George waved his fist in the air. 'Hey! Get your own treats...'

'Oi George!' It was Toby. 'Not much luck in there. Are you OK?'

'Yeah. Did you see that? One of the Bradley twins nicked my cake!'

Olivia and Pali came out of the pub, clutching half eaten packets of crisps and peanuts. Olivia offered them to George.

'Thanks, it'll make up for that Bradley idiot nicking my cake.'

As if on cue, Ben and Billy Bradley tumbled out of the pub. They were dressed in matching orange pumpkin costumes and could just about fit through the doorway. 'What you talking about fatso? We haven't nicked anything of yours...yet.'

Olivia pointed her broomstick at Ben and then

swiftly prodded him in the stomach. 'Leave George alone. Shoo!'

Ben sneered at Olivia. 'You don't scare me.'

Toby pulled at Olivia's long black cloak. 'Come on. Let's go to the Halloween party. It's started, I can hear music.'

Ben chuckled. 'Hey look Billy! It's a ginger vampire. Thought we told you to leave Mappleford freckles?'

George nudged Pali. 'Watch this. Pumpkin tackle practise!'

George dived at the Bradley twins, sending two giant pumpkins rolling down the street towards the village hall.

The village hall was starting to fill up and Mrs Mac the school dinner lady was in charge of taking the money at the door.

George was bouncing the Bradley twins against the wall. 'That's for pinching my cake! I don't know how you got out of that zombie costume so quickly, but I know it was one of you two!'

'What's going on out there?' Mrs Mac shouted. 'Sensible queuing faces please. No pushing.'

Inside the village hall, monsters and ghouls from all over Mappleford were gyrating to the beat of the disco and munching on tiny sausages on sticks. Toby was relieved to see that the Bradley twins had been distracted by the lure of abandoned drinks and George's attention was fully on the buffet.

There was a sudden loud hissing noise and a voice boomed over the music. 'Ladies and Gentlemen, please may I have your attention. It is with great pleasure...hiccup... that I welcome you all to the Mappleford Halloween party...hiccup.'

Olivia groaned. It was her father, Captain Uthers-Freemonty.

'As you know, it is my duty as Lord of the Manor House...hiccup... to provide the prize for the best Halloween costume. This year the prize is a slap up meal for four at the village pub. No expense spared. So, please do join me...hiccup... on the stage now for the judging to begin.'

George adjusted his mask, pulled down his t-shirt and elbowed his way through the crowd towards the stage. Pali and Olivia followed him. 'Come on Toby! One of us could win.'

Toby was about to follow when he noticed the curtains move at the side of the stage. He stood still, waiting for them to twitch again. He was sure that it wasn't his imagination. The heavy curtains flapped and there he was, standing in the wings of the stage, the zombie.

'Ah there you are Toby. I've been looking everywhere for you.' It was Toby's mum. She linked his arm and ushered him towards a crowded table in the corner of the room. 'There's someone I want you to meet.'

Toby reluctantly followed his mum. He looked over his shoulder, trying to spot the zombie. He wasn't in the wings anymore. He was on the stage and standing behind Olivia.

'Olivia, don't turn around. There's a zombie behind you.'

'Pali, it's a Halloween party; the room is full of zombies.' Olivia looked behind her and smiled. 'It's only Badger Fred silly.'

Badger Fred was the groundsman at the Manor House and had earned his nickname on account of his black bushy eyebrows and mop of white hair.

'Are you sure? That blood looks real to me.'

'Of course I'm sure. He told me he was coming as a zombie.'

Pali turned his head and nodded at Badger Fred, not wanting to appear rude. Dark, empty eyes glared back at him and Pali suddenly felt a chill.

Captain Uthers-Freemonty placed the microphone to his mouth. 'Ladies and Gents, boys and girls, we are pleased to announce that we have a winner. And we are delighted to invite our very own pub landlady...hiccup...Mrs Bradley, on stage to present the prize.'

## Chilled to the Bone

Mrs Bradley's large frame tottered onto the stage. She looked every inch the wicked witch with her crooked nose and warty face. She clutched a gold envelope and smiled at her waiting audience. The Bradley twins bounced with delight.

Billy prodded George in his overstretched ribs, hard. 'If our ma's judging, we're bound to win. You're a loser fatso.'

George ignored him and watched as Mrs Bradley prepared to make her announcement. She flicked her green wig out of her eyes and cleared her throat.

'Come on! Get on with it! We haven't got all night!' Someone shouted.

Mrs Bradley flashed a warning look into the crowd before tearing the envelope open. 'The winner of this year's Mappleford Halloween Mask competition...is...Badger Fred!'

Everyone, apart from two giant pumpkins and a fat skeleton, clapped as a walking white sheet made its way onto the stage.

'Fix! It's a fix!' Ben and Billy shouted.

Olivia leaned in close to Pali. 'If Badger Fred is dressed as a ghost...who's the zombie behind us?'

'Dunno...is it still there?'

Olivia slowly turned her head. A red-faced devil grinned back at her and Olivia let out a loud shriek.

The vicar took off his mask and smiled. 'It's OK my child. It's only me…'

Olivia silently put a spell on the grinning vicar before clutching Pali's arm. 'No, it's gone. Perhaps Badger Fred got changed into a ghost costume?'

'Or perhaps it wasn't Badger Fred.'

'If it's not Badger Fred, then who is it?'

Olivia shrugged her shoulders and followed the crowd of monster misfits off the stage.

After rescuing Toby from a plump female Ogre with crooked teeth and bad skin, George announced that he was bored.

Pali held up an abandoned papier-mâché leg. 'We could play hide the severed limb?'

Olivia shook her head. 'Or, we could go for a Halloween walk?'

George sighed. 'Boring...'

'Not if it's through the graveyard.'

George slapped the witch on the back. 'Now you're talking. Come on, no-one will even notice that we've gone.'

Pali protested but was promptly shoved out of the door and into the dark night.

Silhouetted by the glowing full moon, a vampire, werewolf, witch and a skeleton ran through the village of Mappleford, totally unaware that they were being followed by two giant pumpkins.

Olivia led the way down the deserted path that cut through the graveyard. 'See, there's nothing to be scared of,' she said.

Pali wasn't so sure. 'It's creepy. Let's just stay close together. I don't want to get separated. Toby...Toby where are you?'

Toby stood behind a large gravestone. 'Over here! You've got to see this! It's a freshly dug grave.'

George grinned at Olivia. 'Or a freshly *opened* grave...'

'George you do talk utter nonsense sometimes...are you suggesting that some dead person has escaped from their grave?'

'Not a person...a zombie!'

At that very moment the church bells rang out, crashing into the silence of the night. 'It's midnight! Get out of here!'

They raced through the graveyard as fast as their costumes would allow. Suddenly, they all skidded to a halt. The zombie they had seen earlier was slumped against a headstone. George tapped it lightly with his foot. It didn't move.

Olivia hid behind Toby. 'George!'

'He's just drunk. Although...' George bent down to take a closer look at the zombie's face. 'We could take off his mask and see who it is...'

George ran his fingers over the grey puckered

face, feeling for the edge of the mask. Pali, Olivia and Toby bent down to get a closer look.

'George, do hurry up...'

George looked up at his friends. 'Errr...there's something you should know...'

'Yes George?'

'It's not...'

'Yes George?'

'It's not...'

The zombie's eyes flashed open and it grabbed at George's ankles. 'It's not a mask! RUN!'

Screaming, they dashed for the gate and sprinted out of the graveyard...and straight into the Bradley twins.

'What are you lot up to?'

George blurted. 'Don't go in there! There's a zombie in there!'

'Yeah, right. Come on Billy. Let's show these losers that they can't scare us.'

Olivia began to protest but Toby put his hand over her mouth. 'Shush.'

Ben and Billy laughed as they boldly stomped through the graveyard in their pumpkin outfits. 'See!' Ben shouted. 'There's nothing to be scared of!'

George grinned. 'Come on, let's leave them to it and get back to the party.'

They were just pushing their way through the

departing crowds at the village hall when an eerie howling noise filled the air.

The red faced devil put his hand on Toby's shoulder. 'What was that?'

Toby grinned. 'Nothing to worry about vicar. It's just a zombie eating two giant pumpkins.'

The devil chuckled as he made his way back to the vicarage.

© Sharon Hopwood 2015

## Dance Macabre

Gathering in the graveyard on a raw, wintry night
Underneath St Bardolph's crumbling tower
Watching as the hands creep past the sticking minutes
To meet at the midnight hour.
Up jumps the Patterman, in red from horns to heels
He's paid the fiddlers – now he calls the tune
Welcome all you pilgrims from the Deep Six Estate
Here to dance by the glitter ball moon.
Let's dance!

*Jack of Diamonds, Ace of Spades*
*Grab those ghouls and promenade*
*All join hands and circle to the south*
*Spit those maggots outta yor mouth*
*Choose your partners and form a square*
*Vampires here and zombies there*

(to the tune of Yankee Doodle)
*Jack the Ripper came to town*
*On the Eve of Hallows*
*Turned the ladies' insides out*
*But still escaped the gallows*

*Allemande left with your corner girl*
*Bite her neck then give her a whirl*
*Big foot up and little foot down*
*Shake the bag of bones and spin her around*
*She don't smell sweet but what the hell*
*Formaldehyde just ain't Chanel.*
*Let's dance!*

Jigging round the tombstones in a long, jagged, line.
Blue jeans and chequered shirts in tattered rags
Rotting boots and skirts hang from mould-encrusted bones
Dead men dance with the midnight hags.
Fiddlers scrape the tune out on strings from gutless cats
Their fleshless fingers glow a bloodless white.
Up jumps the Patterman and urges them, play on
Come dance with the Devil tonight.
Let's dance!

*Do si do with Lizzie but don't relax*
*She killed her Momma with a big, sharp axe*
*Promenade the vamp with her petticoat a floppin'*
*Shoe fell off and a hole's in her stockin'*
*Swing with Mary and swing with Rose*
*Elbow hook the witch with a wart on her nose.*

## Chilled to the Bone

(to the tune of Yankee Doodle)
*In this town they light a fire*
*On the Eve of Hallows*
*Then queue to see the witches burn*
*While toasting their marshmallows*

*Four zombies chain and don't be slow*
*Kiss the caller before you go*
*Sashay to your partners and swing them round*
*'Til the holes in their heads make a whistling sound*
*Werewolf in the corner chewing on a bone*
*Sorry folks, it's time to go home.*

Gathering in the graveyard now as silent as the tomb
Gazing at the ancient, sacred tower
Sighing as the hands speed past the fleeting minutes
To meet at the day's first hour.
Down goes the Patterman and waves a fond goodbye
A single chime from Bardolph's rusted bell
Farewell to you pilgrims from the Deep Six Estate
Another year awaits you all in Hell
Let's go!

*A right and a left around the ring*

## Bardstown Writers

*Before the roosters crow and the sparrows sing*
*Promenade home now side by side*
*Like a knock-kneed groom and a bow-legged bride*
*Good girls walk and bad girls ride*
*Come on, Lizzie, the hearse is outside.*
*Let's go!*

(to the tune of Yankee Doodle)
*Dance with strangers if you dare*
*When October's midnight moon glows*
*The Patterman is in your town*
*Calling on the Eve of Hallows*

© Pam Pattison 2015

# The Lake at Foxcote

Richard unwrapped the remaining item in the tea chest with care and placed it in a prominent position on his bedside table.

'There you are Anne, my love, back with me again,' he whispered, as he tenderly pressed his lips to the glass.

He loved this photograph of his wife, taken not long after they had met. Her evident vitality brought the cruelty of her death to the forefront of his mind, not that he ever stopped thinking about her. He reflected on the anguish he had suffered as a consequence of losing her. He hadn't felt this wretched since their son, Jonathan, had been killed all those years ago. Moving to Foxcote Cottage was a fresh start, although he still felt battered by grief. His friends thought he had been foolish to choose such an uninhabited place, but at present he craved peace and solitude.

He glanced out of the window and, noticing that the light was fading, realised he faced a long, dark evening alone. It was Halloween but he wouldn't be opening his door to the laughing cry of 'Trick-or-Treat?' this year. Nonetheless he reminded himself of his vow that he wouldn't shun human company entirely and decided to make his first appearance at the pub. After all, he might bump into Brian, his nearest neighbour who seemed friendly, and he suspected that a chat with Brian would lift his mood.

Foxcote Cottage was surrounded by private woodland belonging to Foxcote House and later that evening Richard set out along the track that led to the village. As soon as he was engulfed by the darkness of the woods he become aware of an appalling smell – the unmistakeable stench of dirty, stagnant water – although his torchlight revealed nothing. How odd, he thought. He'd better watch where he was stepping.

Immediately he sensed something stir close by and shone his torch towards the sound. Expecting to see the receding rump of a startled deer, he was shocked when the light revealed a woman with a small boy clinging to her.

'Anne! Jonathan!' Richard shouted impulsively, but the woman disappeared behind the trees. She yanked the boy so roughly that he stumbled over her long skirt as it dragged along the ground.

Richard resisted the compulsion to pursue them as he knew he could get himself into trouble. He had imagined seeing Anne once before – since her death. After all he hadn't had a clear look at them. She was probably a woman from the village, although it was late for her to be in this isolated woods with such a young lad. Their appearance had been strangely old-fashioned and they were inappropriately dressed for this cold weather. Perhaps they were returning from a Halloween party and had lost their way.

The incident was over so quickly that he began to doubt that he had seen this odd pairing at all – maybe he was hallucinating, as his longing for Anne was so intense. God! He could still smell that awful stench. He wasn't imagining that!

Although unnerved he decided to persevere with his plan. As he entered 'The Silent Woman', he was comforted by the warmth of the open fire and the general mood of conviviality. Brian was seated at the bar and shouted across to him. 'Richard! Good to see you. What will it be?'

They moved to a table by the window and, emboldened by a few gulps of beer, Richard felt able to tell Brian what he had just experienced. To Richard's amazement Brian wasn't dismissive, but rather his expression became troubled as he said, 'If you're going to remain at Foxcote Cottage, Richard, I must tell you the legend of 'The Lake at Foxcote.' Have you visited the lake yet?'

But Brian carried on without waiting for Richard's response. 'It's a beautiful, atmospheric, almost hypnotic place within the grounds of Foxcote House. Although the lake is small, the water is deep – dangerously deep. A line of ancient willow trees guide you to it and, when obscured by the mist that often hangs over the lake, they can be mistaken for motionless figures standing with their heads drooping, looking for all the world like mourners at a funeral.'

'I haven't found the lake yet, but I hope to go tomorrow,' Richard replied. 'I try to walk every day as I have a few health problems – a weak heart, I'm afraid. I assume the public footpath…'

'In that case, I must tell you this now,' Brian interrupted abruptly. 'Tomorrow, All Hallows' Day, is the anniversary of a tragic event that has haunted, indeed blighted, this area for one hundred years. Legend has it that, as the temperatures were unseasonably mild, John, the elder son of Lord Foxcote, who was only three years old, had been taken by his nursemaid to picnic beside the lake. A disagreement broke out between them as he was misbehaving and she was frightened that he was going to fall in. She moved to grab him but he dodged her grasp, and did indeed lose his balance and plunge headlong into the lake. Her screams were heard by his father, out shooting on the estate, who rushed over and jumped into the freezing depths to rescue his boy. The Estate Manager also tore over and pulled Lord Foxcote from the lake but he was in a terrible condition. He was rushed to the House but, although the doctor was called, it was too late, he couldn't be saved. He had suffered heart failure. As if that wasn't enough, it was inexplicable, but the little boy's body was never recovered. The nursemaid never spoke again, and was swiftly removed to an asylum. A child is said to haunt this area with a pale woman destined to stay close by his side, watching and protecting him, as if atoning for her one moment of neglect.'

After a pause, Brian looked Richard directly in the eyes and said, 'These heart-rending events are destined to be repeated every hundred years, and always on All Hallows' Day.'

'My God, Brian, what an awful story. Do you mean to say that I have just seen them in the woods... that they were spectres?'

'Well yes, don't you?' asked Brian, tersely.

'Yes, I suppose so. But... I can't help wondering...,' started Richard, his head in his hands.

'Yes?'

'But I can't help thinking that maybe it's Anne ... I mean ... maybe I was meant to come here... maybe she's trying to contact me. We had a little boy too, who... who was killed.'

'Well, I don't know Richard...'

'I must go to the lake tomorrow, to see what

happens… just in case. Otherwise, I'll never be able to rest.'

'Yes, well, if you put it like that…'

Richard left 'The Silent Woman' towards closing time and, feeling disturbed by Brian's tale, walked the long way home to avoid the woods. The evening had been very upsetting and not the positive experience he had been hoping for.

After a sleepless night, although Richard hadn't dismissed Brian's story entirely, he also hadn't abandoned his frantic hope that Anne was trying to reach him. So he pinpointed the lake on the map and, before the sun had fully appeared, strode off on a route that would take him directly to it.

Richard blundered along the unkempt footpaths until he saw a pair of willow trees in the distance. He knew straight away that they announced the former path of the river and the presence of the lake. As he drew nearer, he noticed that a low mist hung over the lake so that he could only just make out a sign that read 'Danger – Deep Water.' He was struck by how silent and still everything seemed – just the sort of retreat he yearned for; usually.

Then suddenly his attention was gripped by a woman and little boy picnicking beside the lake. They had their backs to him but he was certain that they were the same figures that he had glimpsed in the woods the previous evening. It was still bitterly cold and yet a feast was spread out on a blanket as though it was a balmy summer's day. As he watched in horror, the events that Brian had narrated started to play out in front of him. The little boy stood up and staggered towards the water's edge. The woman lunged forward as if to take hold of his arm, but he jerked it away. As he did so, he lost his footing and there was a dull thud as he entered the water – hardly even a splash. The woman started screaming. Deep down Richard knew that these events were not real; they were not really happening here and now, but how could he stand by while a young lad drowned in front of his eyes? The water would be freezing, he had a weak heart – but should that stop him trying to rescue an innocent boy?

He could hear Brian calling him, but the voice seemed faint, as if Brian was standing at the end of a long tunnel. Why was Brian coming? In any case it would take too long for him to arrive. Richard knew he must act.

'Jon! Jon! Hang on, Daddy's coming!' he yelled as he flung down his rucksack, fumbled to remove his walking boots and dived into the icy water.

On the day of Richard's funeral, Brian was the first to arrive at the church and he took his seat towards the rear. He picked up the Order of Service and was absentmindedly looking at the photograph of Richard on the front cover, when he sensed a chilling presence, coupled with a disgusting reek of putrid water. He lifted his head slowly and his gaze locked onto the watery eyes of a pale woman with a small boy clinging to her skirts. They exchanged gloating, triumphant smiles.

© Elizabeth Cox 2015

# Old Pumpkin Head

His real name was Joe, but in time we called him 'Old Pumpkin Head', and that was probably one of the kinder names we gave him. Kids can be pretty cruel. Even now though, I reckon he lived up to his name. I haven't seen him for years. I find it hard to forget him.

It was his bright orange hair that gave him his name; it sprouted in all directions from the top of his round head. And there were freckles, loads of them, all scattered across his snub nose like brown confetti. And I hadn't better forget his teeth either; they had wide gaps between them and they loomed out from his wide mouth which was turned up like he had fish-hooks in each corner. So over all, he was a funny looking bloke, and he did look like a Halloween pumpkin.

As my mate Charlie said with a snigger: 'I reckon he's an alien and if he is then his parents must look really weird.' Me? Well I just I reckoned he was a little simple but I probably can't say that these days though, it's just not politically correct. Or as my Mum would have said: 'It's not polite either.'

Joe arrived in our school one day without any warning. He'd got out of a car and was there in the classroom before we knew it. The teacher introduced him, and we all gaped and gazed at him as only kids can do. He didn't say much; just kept his big orange head down and tried to be invisible. We never saw his parents collect him after school; I guess like him, they kept themselves to themselves.

Joe couldn't escape us, he had to come to school, and I still cringe when I remember some of the things we did and said to him. We didn't mean to hurt him I'm sure, but you know how it is with kids; one thing leads to another and before you know it you're doing something that you'd shudder at if you were an adult. He never retaliated; just seemed to take it on the chin.

At the end of the day he always raced out of the school yard. We were too busy fooling around to notice that he'd gone. The only time we ever saw him outside school hours was once when he drove past in his parent's car; he stared out of the back seat window looking like a gingerbread man in a jar.

We had an idea where he lived - out on a small development a mile or so away. Some people said that the houses had sprouted overnight and it became known to us as 'The Sprouts.' We never went back to his place, and we never took him back to ours either.

## Chilled to the Bone

It was early on Halloween that some of us decided to play a real trick on him; something we reckoned would really scare him. We followed him home late that afternoon as the mist was coming down and the leaves gathered beneath the chestnut trees. We giggled our twelve-year old giggles as we nipped from hedge to hedge so that he wouldn't see us if he turned around.

We arrived in The Sprouts before we knew it - one moment we were in the lane and the next we turned a corner and there they were; six brand new, tall and narrow houses with pointed roofs, each with a dormer window. Funny, but there weren't any people there and no cars on any of the short driveways, just half a dozen identical houses and some big trees overhanging the pavement.

Joe trotted onto one of the driveways, and by the time we got anywhere near his place he had gone inside. It was getting dark now and as there weren't any street lights we began to feel nervous. Whose idea it was to try and scare the living daylights out of him on Halloween, I can't remember. I was dressed as a skeleton, and the others were witches, ghouls and ghosts and there was even a Dracula lookalike complete with red lines coming from his mouth.

We bunched together in the shadows of one of the big trees and looked at the house that Joe had gone into - we held on to each other in the dark. Suddenly a rectangle of light snapped on in the dormer window and we could see Joe moving in the orange light of what must have been his room. Funny, but his head looked bigger than ever. Charlie the ghoul said 'He looks just like a pumpkin,' and that was when the name stuck. One of the ghosts chuckled 'Old Pumpkin Head' and we all laughed softly. Then Charlie pulled the elastic back on his catapult and fired a pebble straight at the window.

It sounded like a pistol shot when it smacked into the wall next to the window and that was when things became really scary. Joe came to the window and glared down at us with blazing eyes - they weren't his normal eyes, this time they were red, bright red, and his face was almost black with fury. Looking back it's like all the anger that he'd been building up over the way we had treated him was now burning away through his eyes at us. Maybe tonight was the final straw.

Dracula was the first to move. He jumped out of the shadows and began to prance around shouting at Joe; pretty soon we were all doing the same, calling him names and throwing things at his house. Joe stared at us even more intently and he stood at the window with his hands below the sill.

Then the ground began to tremble and with a loud splitting and grinding rumble the house lifted into the air, hovered for a moment then slowly turned on its axis. We could see Joe, he looked like a pilot in his cockpit as he tilted the house until the gable top was pointing straight at us. Then, just a few feet above the ground, it moved inexorably towards us.

We ran in sheer terror, our strangled cries splitting the early night. Each time we looked back the house was silently following like a huge arrow head, and worse than that, a couple more of the houses were following suit. We stumbled our way out towards the safety of the distant glare of our village's street lights, and finally gathered, wild-eyed and gasping for breath under one of them. Cautiously we looked back. All was quiet. Somehow and somewhere the terror had disappeared and after a while we dispersed.

I went straight to my room, didn't even speak to my Mum who wanted to know where I'd been; just grunted as I closed my door. I hardly slept that night and in the darkness I promised that I would look for Joe the following morning and apologise to him and see if I could make up for all the cruel things we did to him.

But we never saw him again. The teacher told us that his family had suddenly moved. A week or so later we went gingerly back to The Sprouts to see if what we had seen that night was true. The trees were still there, pushing out over the pavement. But not only were there were no people, there were no houses; no sign of there ever having been any - the ground where they had stood was now flat and looked undisturbed. It was like they had never been there.

I grew up a bit that Halloween but even now, decades later, I'm still embarrassed at my behaviour and wish that instead of following the crowd I'd made more of an effort to befriend Joe.

And I'd still love to know how he flew that house.

© Tim Binder 2015

# Unwanted

'Not a pretty sight.' I tried to lighten the situation for our trainee, Emma, who'd never seen a face rearranged into a bloody, Picasso-like pulp.

She usually worked with James. I'd watch them flirting above the dead.

James wasn't in today.

An IC1 male, approximately forty, with no ID. The intact eyeball, clinging to the corpse, was blue.

Like James's.

Taking a scalpel, I allowed my hand to linger on hers. She pulled away as if burnt.

'Don't!'

'I'm so sorry.'

*He* did all that touchy, feely stuff.'

'James?'

'Yes.'

'I thought... you two?'

'I loved him.'

'Oh.'

'I wanted him, not this.' She clutched her abdomen. 'Neither did he.'

'He'll come round.'

She emitted a bizarre, high-pitched laugh.

'Not from this he won't.'

*Oh.* I began backing away.

The blow, expertly placed, struck the left ventricular chamber. I sank to the floor while, in my head, I was transcribing the post-mortem.

© JJ Franklin

# Skin Treatment

The terrible thing about the unknown is that it goes on for ever. Exorcise one demon and you can never be sure that its malignant relatives won't follow, even centuries later. But, on the surface, the house Polly and Leo were about to buy was a perfectly ordinary 1930s semi. Hardly a haven for restless spirits.

True the church was just round the corner, so if you think tombstones are spooky, you could imagine transparent wraiths floating about on a moonless night. On the other hand, a tombstone at least indicates that somebody blessed the buried body, however imperfect the life it had led.

Not that the estate agent was trying to hide anything when he took them round for their first viewing in April. Although it had been a global warming sort of day, Polly had shivered as they went up the narrow flight of stairs into the roof extension and she stumbled on the top step.

'Are you all right, Mrs Sadler?' he had asked, putting it down to the fact that she was pregnant. He clearly did not expect a reply as he went immediately into his spiel about the advantages of having a roof extension with double-glazed Velux windows – so much free light coming in and not an expensive therm escaping.

The house was on a corner, the last of a row of conventional semis – the very embodiment of English suburban aspiration of its time, the inappropriate fake Tudor beams under the gables picked out in black against white pebbledash. Nothing threatening there, then, unless you happen to be an architect.

But the minute Polly stepped into the attic room with its sloping ceiling she felt uneasy. It was no more than a prickle at the back of her neck which made her shiver, and not important enough to make a fuss about. After all, they couldn't afford to be too picky. The asking price was lower than the average for the street because the executors wanted a quick sale and in any case, the roof room would be a perfect place to leave her paints and canvases without cluttering up the rest of the house and making it smell of turps.

It was so obviously a studio that she had not been surprised, when she first saw it, that several pictures had been left on the walls. She didn't look at them in detail, but the immediate impression was of a lot of gold leaf and black squiggles. 'Leo – come and look at these,' she called down the stairwell but when she turned back the pictures had gone, the walls were bare and there was a faint smell of bleach. The vision had been so vivid she shook her head as if this would bring the pictures back. She had seen the room as a studio and studios are full of pictures. That was all. In any case, Leo had been talking figures to the agent and hadn't heard her.

The move went smoothly enough and they managed to decant the cardboard boxes quite quickly. The odd thing, which they hadn't expected when they first viewed the house, was that all their belongings fitted perfectly. There seemed to be plugs just where they wanted to put lamps, shelves which were perfect for their bits and pieces, cupboards that accommodated all their clothes. It was almost as if they had lived there before and were just returning after a holiday.

Polly set up her easel in the room under the roof and Leo, who was a freelance tax consultant and did a lot of work at home, used the spare bedroom, directly below the studio, as a study. He was always so absorbed in his laptop that the movements above didn't bother him – Polly always walked backwards and forwards as she was painting.

Occasionally, when he heard the footsteps change from a clack on the bare studio stairs to a soft pad on the carpeted treads to the hall, he shouted down to Polly to say that if she was making a cup of coffee for herself, could she bring him one? When no coffee appeared he didn't think anything of it. He just assumed she was finding two flights of stairs more difficult as her bump reached its seventh month. He didn't do imagination.

The baby was due at the end of October and Polly's blood pressure meant that she had to rest. Trudging up two flights of stairs made her breathless. She also found that when she did venture up to the studio the baby kicked so much it was actually painful. She spent tedious afternoons lying on the sofa, not quite watching afternoon TV and listening to intermittent creaks that sounded as if the house were breathing – a bit like an old building with joists and beams that wheezed when the weather changed. Not at all like a solidly dependable, three-up-two-down, pre-war semi. Above her, Leo seemed to be as unsettled as the house and more than once she fancied he went up to the studio, she couldn't think why.

The next time she heard him come downstairs she listened to his steps go down the hall to the kitchen and was about to call out to him when she heard him open the door to the glazed patio and go down a further flight of stairs. It was then she began to think that pregnancy had addled her brain. The house had no cellar.

She froze, holding her breath as the footsteps

returned, padded up the stairs to the studio, down to the first floor, then to the ground floor and then down a non-existent staircase to the non-existent cellar. The soles flapped quietly against bare heels, more like soft sandals than boots or shoes. Backwards and forwards. Up and down. Fetching and carrying.

'Leo!' It was a shriek, rather than a call.

He opened his study door. 'What's the matter?'

'There's somebody in the house!'

He ran downstairs, through the open patio doors into the garden and then round the side of the house to the front, coming back to hold her tightly.

'There isn't anybody there. You've been dreaming.'

'I haven't. Really I haven't. Something was moving under the floorboards. Could it have been an animal? Was there a farm or something here before these houses were built?'

'I should think it was open fields originally. It was probably church land, so maybe the priests used it to grow vegetables. There must be some archives somewhere. I'll have a look in the morning.'

She lay awake for hours that night and when she did sleep she dreamed of catacombs piled with gilded skulls. When Leo went round to look at the parish records the next day, she felt nervous at being left alone. The baby was really uncomfortable and seemed to be turning in its….. in its…. she couldn't finish her thought.

He was gone for several hours, but when he returned he was triumphant. He had made scrupulous notes from the records. He loved facts.

'Look what I found,' he said. 'There used to be a group of priests here in the late 13th century. They sang Mass for the souls of the dead in a chapel where the parish hall is now, and they lived just the other side of our back garden wall. There was an underground passage that led to the chantry.

'Listen to this – it's a great story. There were outbuildings on this corner where we are. One of the priests was a wonderful artist, so although all four slept in a dormitory, an upstairs room was set aside specially for him. There he could make illuminated manuscripts of the church history. He made his own vellum by treating calf skins with lime and bleaching them. He scraped them with a curved knife to make them thin and stretched them on a frame.

'One day one of the choristers went missing and was never seen again. There was a bit of hullabaloo because the boy had helped the illuminator to sharpen his quills, grind minerals and boil plants to make pigments and some of the locals thought that was not all he did to help. But they didn't dare speak of their suspicions and eventually the boy was forgotten by everyone but his mother.

'Years later there was a huge fire in the workroom and the four priests spent all night trudging to and from the studio and down to the underground passage, trying to save the unfinished manuscripts. There was one manuscript that the artist refused to let anyone else touch. He carried it out himself and then went back through the flames and smoke for a metal chest, which he dragged out into the garden before the whole building exploded in a ball of fire. All the manuscripts were destroyed, apart from the one he had saved.

'It's still in the church, in a sealed glass case. The colours are particularly vibrant because they are painted on a smoother base than usual and nobody knows what skin the artist had cut and stretched to make the vellum. Until then, the most malleable skin was of a still-born goat, but this skin is as soft and smooth as a child's.

'It wasn't until builders started digging the foundations for our row of houses about eighty-five years ago that they found the metal box. It contained a whole load of ground-up pigments and gold leaf and a curved knife. Anything else had completely disintegrated, apart from one thing – a complete skeleton of a small boy curled up like a foetus.'

'How horrible,' said Penny. 'Is it true?'

'Probably not. The footnotes say there isn't any proof. But do you know the strangest thing?'

'What?'

'The priest who is supposed to have murdered the child. He was real enough. He's in the records. His name was Father Leofrick and he came from a family of saddlers. He died in 1313 and you'll never guess his birthday.'

Penny felt the baby kick violently. 'I think I can,' she said grimly. 'I'd put money on October 31st.'

© Beryl Louise Downing 2015

# Don't Open the Attachment!

My husband always said I was next to useless with computers. It's ironic really, given that I make my living writing articles for magazines. I just need to get this one finished and then I'm off to bed, not before time as well. I'm looking forward to being wrapped up in my blanket, the log on the fire is about finished and I can already feel the room starting to get cold. I'm certainly not going to put another on the fire now, writing articles for magazines isn't that well paid, I'm afraid. There we go, last few words finished and now to mail it off to the editor. I promised her I would have it to her tonight.

I see some emails have dropped in the inbox, I'll just take a quick look at them before closing down for the night. Shouldn't really, I can feel the warm duvet waiting for me but it might be something important. I don't think I'll even bother with a warm drink tonight, just straight up those stairs to Beddington as my mother used to say all those years ago. There are a couple of adverts and some general junk to delete. What would I want with a fake Rolex at my age?

There is one interesting one, from a fellow writer asking me to take a look at a piece of work for them. Can't say I recall the name but I remember when I was starting out, always appreciated a few words of advice from a friend or colleague. Shouldn't really, this can wait till the morning, my eyes are drooping. Reg always said to be careful opening files you weren't sure about, but he isn't here now so he'll just have to roll in his grave. Besides, it'll be my bedtime reading if I can keep my eyes open.

I'm double clicking on the attachment but not much is happening, just a little black box with some letters flying past and then nothing. Oh well, all a bit much to be worrying about tonight, maybe I should have left it alone after all.

*Hello.* A small green bubble pops up in the corner of my computer screen.

I have no idea where that came from and it's certainly nothing I should be interested in. My grand-daughter does all this texting and talking to people on the computer but not me. I prefer the real world, what's the point of writing something down when you can say it out loud. That's funny, especially coming from a person who writes for a living.

*Do you want to talk?*

Not really, I think, and quickly click the small 'x' above the bubble. I won't be doing any of that tonight and go to lower the screen of my laptop, shutting off the computer for the night, or at least putting it to sleep. Not the only one who needs a bit of sleep, I think.

*Don't go, I just want to chat a bit.*

Enough of this nonsense, time to switch off this blessed machine properly and get to bed. I watch as the closing down screen appears and then the black, slightly mirror-like, screen confirms that everything is off.

*That was a bit rude.*

The bubble pops up in the middle of the screen, causing a short and involuntary intake of breath. I could have sworn the computer was shut off, I saw it close down.

*Yes, I know, clever isn't it?* Another bubble pops up, replacing the one before.

Underneath the bubble there is a flashing cursor, for me to input my answer or reply. I don't want to, everything tells me to leave it and go upstairs to bed but I know I'll never rest. How can I rest with this going on? It's only a bit of nonsense on a computer but it'll be on my mind, I know what I'm like and I'll be thinking about it all night.

*I only want to talk.*

The cursor flashes as I look at the screen, begging me to input a reply, begging me to acknowledge whoever this is. I don't want to, I just want to leave it and go upstairs to my bed. The log on the fire has now burnt out completely and it's turned quite chilly in here.

*Please don't ignore me*, the bubble pops up again. *I don't like it when you ignore me.*

The flashing cursor is too tempting. I want to get this all over so I can go to sleep for the night.

'What do you want?' I type slowly, my fingers shaking as I do.

*I told you, I just want to talk.*

'Why?' I type, confused as to why this was happening here and now, last thing at night while I sit alone on my sofa.

**_I'm here to warn you._** The bubble pops up again, with the words underlined, stressing the importance of this message.

'Warn me?' There is something unnerving about the way the previous message is bold and underlined. It's as if there is something immediate and urgent this person is trying to tell me.

*Warn you to not open the door.*

Why would someone, from wherever, warn me not to open the door? At this time of night, when everyone else would be tucked up warm in their beds, just like I was looking forward to being. I lift my finger to type but, just as I am about to touch the first letter of my reply, the familiar ring of my front door echoes around the house. The sound cracks the silence, snapping me away from the isolation of my computer screen. Every muscle in my body tenses instantaneously and my mouth opens to scream, though no sound comes out.

***I warned you, don't answer it.*** The letters in the bubble on my screen are larger now, bold and red in colour.

I can hear the sound of my breath and can feel a cold sweat breaking out on my brow and under the neck of my jumper.

'I don't know who you are but stop now.' I shout out loud, not taking time to think if anybody can hear me; maybe I am trying to talk to whoever is on the other side of my front door at this ungodly hour.

*You'll need to type it.* The bubble pops up again. *I can only hear you when you type it.*

My heart racing, I steady my fingers and press out my next message. Too scared now, too scared to touch type, so I tap away with my two index fingers. Reg would be grumbling if he could see this, *what was the point of all those typing classes if you're not going to use what you learned?*

'Stop it now, stop it. I'm calling the police!!' I thump out, with rage now flowing through my fingertips. I take a moment to raise a cracked smile at my using two exclamation marks; my creative writing teacher would definitely have something to say about that. Two exclamation marks are the equivalent of laughing at your own jokes, that's what he used to say.

Silence falls on the room but I cannot move, I wonder where the person is who's rung the front door and why this is happening to me. I lift myself from my seat and walk over to the telephone, checking my steps as I walk, I've been sitting down too long, I'm all a bit stiff and tingly now. Circulation these days not quite what it was. My heart is thumping out of my chest, if I look down I feel I will see it pounding against the inside of my red jumper.

In the corner of the room the phone receiver rests, waiting for me to pick it up and call the local police station. What will I say? That my computer is threatening me? That somebody has rung the door in the middle of the night? That I am just terrified and I want someone to come out and tell me everything is OK? I stretch out my arm, watching it shake uncontrollably, reaching to pick up the receiver. The shrill ring of the telephone halts me just as I am about to lift it. I stare at the telephone, confused and terrified as to why it has decided to ring at this moment. It continues to ring, my head wants to scream at it to stop but I pick it up and listen.

'Hello, Mrs Strickland? This is the police, we're

just returning the call you made.' I can't speak, my mouth too dry, my brain racing too quick to think what to say. 'Is everything all right? We just wanted to check that everything was OK.'

'Please come, please come now. 46 Isaac Row. Please.' My words are quiet, stilted, panicked. I can feel a small tear rolling down my cheek now, strangely warm against my cold, cold skin.

'Yes, we'll be there in ten minutes. Is everything OK Mrs Strickland?'

'Please. Now.' They are all the words I can find before replacing the receiver and going to sit back on the sofa. My body is still wracked with fear but calm returns as I feel the comfort of knowing the police will be here in less than ten minutes.

*No need to worry.* The bubble pops up on the black screen. *They'll be here soon.*

I look at the screen, the small green bubble sitting alone on the black, unpowered screen. Say what you want, I think, ten minutes from now this will all be over. I stare at the screen but I'm writing nothing now, I'm just sitting here till the police come.

*Before the police do get here, can I send you a picture?*

A further chill crawls up my neck, crawling around my shoulders and forcing my body into an involuntary shiver. I'm not going to answer this, I'll just sit here and wait for the police to come.

They can sort this out for me.

*Please, just one picture. You'll like it, I promise.* The bubble pops up again, I can't pull my eyes away from it but I won't reply to the request, I won't.

*Here it comes.* The bubble pops up and I know that I don't want to see what is about to come but I can't pull my eyes away. My pulse is racing, my skin is dry and it feels like I am sitting in an ice box. There's less than five minutes now, less than five minutes till the police come. It doesn't matter what is on that picture, I only have to sit here for five minutes.

The picture pops up on the computer screen, the computer that I switched off and which shouldn't work. I look at the picture in disbelief, knowing instantly what it is. The back of the head, the brown hair, the red jumper, the green cushions laid out all around her and the computer resting in front of her. Taken from behind, there is no doubt that this picture is of a woman sitting on her sofa late at night, staring at her computer in sheer terror. In the photo behind her, behind me, is the outline of a man, his tattooed hands resting on the back of the sofa, inches from my neck. I can see H-A-T-E inked on both sets of fingers.

*Don't turn around.* The bubble on the computer screen pops up. *Definitely best you don't turn around.*

The flashing of the blue lights of the police car

light up my room, through the curtains, as they pull up outside my house. They are here, but they are too late.

*Ready?* The last green bubble reads as it pops up on the screen.

© Jeff Brades 2015

## Pull Me Close

Pull me close,
Feel my heart beat faster.
Pull me close,
Make my soul sing.
Wrap your arms around me,
Feel,
As tingling bursts through
My skin.
Consume the bliss.
Bathe in the joy.
Share the peace descending,
Which when we are one,
We can bring.
We are joined, you and I,
With that long ago, once given betrothal ring.

You are the light
That warms my glow,
The sweetness to my smell.
I take your hand,
I follow your path,
You make me steady,
Blossom, laugh.
Make me your one,
Your only one,

Make you mine,
And only mine.
Together, we can grow.
Forget false fancies,
Stay honest and true.
Let me fill up your senses.
Let me make you feel new.
Let me flow through your mind.
Be constant, gentle,
Inspiring, and kind.
Your rock in any sea, lean on me,
Your haven in any storm,
I am the flower in your form.

Come to me:
I am yours.
Hold me tight.
Your other half,
Keep me safe,
Keep me in sight.

Your pain will ebb.
Your mist will clear.
We can be day
We can be night.
There will be no more
Torrid, confusing fear,
Only shining, happy, fulfilling light.

## Chilled to the Bone

Now is the moment.
Time has ticked away.
Our door is closing,
Fast, and firmly to.
Someone else waits,
Wanting me,
Biding his cue.
I have a big pick:
As others abound.
But there is folly, there is danger,
Treacherous ground.

It makes me sad,
It makes me sick.
You so far away.
Yet I remain drawn,
Drawn, only to you,
The cord worn away,
But strong and thick,
Despite its fading hue.
Pull me close now,
Pull tight and good.
It's what you want too.
You know you should.

You chose another:
Now I have no choice.
I will stop my calling,

Quieten my voice,
Once I am gone,
(And this time is near),
I will be lost, forever
No more to you dear.
I will blank you out,
Crawl away far,
Snuff our flame,
Put out your star.

Pull me close,
You have broken my heart,
Watch as I drown,
I have fallen apart.

No smile, no laughter, no touch, no looking back.
Setting off, both of us,
Running on opposite, new track.
No return. No being drawn now.
You will not find me.
There will be no how.

I will be forging ahead,
Going alone.
Just a hollow memory,
A ghost, a stone.
Rattling hopelessly around,

## Chilled to the Bone

Echoing in your head.
Beating a drum, distant and dead.
Abandoned, rejected, no more am I
Nothing keeps us together,
There is no more, no beautiful tie.

© Katharine McMaster 2015

# Ghost Seeking

The group gathered cheerfully by the river, giving their money to the tour leader, a rather cadaverous-looking man in top hat and black suit, with an authentic-looking watch chain across his waistcoat. Stage costume cast-offs, the knowledgeable among them nodded to each other. When all the money had been collected, and tickets distributed he climbed up a couple of steps and introduced himself, raising his lantern to light his long face.

'Good evening, ladies and gentlemen, thank you for giving your time, and money, to our celebrated and award-winning ghost tour. For all intents and purposes I am, tonight, Edmund Gravely, a Victorian coffin maker.' He took off the top hat and bowed, his cloak swishing around him.

'We are gathered together on this Halloween evening to look at some of the haunted places of this town, but beware! Some believe that the souls of the departed wander the earth until All Saints' Day, which is tomorrow, and that All Hallows' Eve provides one last chance for the dead to gain vengeance on their enemies before moving to the next world.'

Steve and Jane hugged one another and shivered

in mock alarm. This was their third date, and Steve thought an inspired one. A special late night Halloween ghost tour, what better way to get a girl to cuddle close!

Mr Gravely told them a little story of a small child drowning in the fountain, trying to get to the coins which some people bizarrely threw in as though it was the famous Trevi fountain in Rome. 'Some say her ghost haunts the water - coins move about with no-one near them.'

Saying, 'follow me, if you dare', their guide led them up the road towards the first haunting. 'This house, once a tavern was built sometime in the 1500s and has upwards of 40 ghosts in residence. Many people have reported sightings and strange phenomena. Sorcery, witchcraft and black magic are said to have taken place here. Would you dare to spend the night?' Mr Gravely looked hard at the group, who all shook their heads. He smiled.

As they walked towards the next place, Jane kept close to Steve, nervously looking over her shoulder. 'That place is definitely scary,' she said. Steve put his arm around her.

'Stay close to me and I will save you,' he said

The next inn had stood for many centuries and abounded in ghosts and ghouls, screams and mysterious footsteps.

'Maybe we should check in and spend the night

in the haunted bedroom,' said Steve hopefully.

'Not a chance!' said Jane.

The group moved up the road to another pub, this one haunted by a highwayman who disappeared after being confronted by one of his victims. At the time he was thought to have fled the town, but subsequent sightings throughout the years led to speculation that he had perhaps been murdered for the money and jewels he had stolen, and that his ghost now sought revenge. No one who worked at the pub would go into the side passage after dark, and those unwary visitors who did told of feeling hands tugging at pockets and a coldness, even in the summer. They peered in but none took up Mr Gravely's challenge to enter. Not on this night of all nights.

Jane in particular stood as far as possible from the entranceway and thrilled Steve by clutching him firmly round the middle. 'Oh, yes' he thought. 'Keep those stories coming Mr G.'

Round the corner and they paused outside another timber-framed house. Here, children were heard running up and down the front stairs and people reported hands trying to push them down the back stairs. They gazed at the house, and the lattice windows gazed back. Look! Was that the ghost of the Elizabethan man looking out of the window? Look! Was that a light?

The moon disappeared behind clouds and the street lights dimmed prior to being turned off. They were the only souls in the street, and were suddenly aware of the fact. The hour before the witching hour on All Hallows eve. A breeze started up and they all shivered and moved closer together for comfort and safety.

They moved briskly up the road to the entrance to the churchyard, and huddled around Mr Gravely who told them of the unsolved murder of a woman, whose shade had been seen wandering around the graves. Suddenly he asked them: 'Do any of you believe in ghosts?' Gazing at the tombstones, feeling the chill wind and looking at the dark scudding clouds, most of them nodded and murmured, 'yes.' Steve snorted in disbelief. Mr Gravely looked at him thoughtfully. 'Ah,' he said,' we shall have to see if we can make a believer of you before the night ends.'

Their guide was tall and thin and his voice was deep and dark. Standing next to Steve and close to him, Jane thought Mr Gravely was taller than she'd realised, and she saw his eyes glinting as he looked around the group. She was aware of a musty smell coming from him, and a sort of vibration. He looked at her and she trembled.

More stories of ghostly hauntings and sightings, weeping and wailing followed. Mr Gravely himself seemed more spooky by the minute.

They moved briskly down the road again, then huddled at the bottom of the steps as they heard the tale of the actor who haunted the theatre and was seen before each new production, moving purposely across the stage and disappearing through the backcloth. This happened more often when Macbeth was being played.

Suddenly the tour was over and their guide was thanking them for their attention; the group gradually dispersed. Steve and Jane went towards the river, Mr Gravely followed slowly and thoughtfully in the same direction.

The next morning, frost covered the tombstones and grass in the church cemetery, and covered Steve's battered body, propped against a tree. He was now a believer.

Initial findings indicated a frenzied attack, but only one set of footprints were found around the corpse, and they belonged to the victim. No fingerprints had been found on the nearby lantern.

The police inspector glumly told his sergeant that they would have the devil of a job locating all the people who were in the group the previous night.

'I know, guv, but don't you think it's odd, that the people who regularly run the ghost tours denied having a special late one for Halloween last night?'

When later it was realised that Steve's girlfriend had disappeared, a nationwide hunt was launched. Jane, however, was never seen alive again, but then, neither was Mr Gravely.

© Jann Tracy 2015

## Treat or Trick?

The village of Minchford nestled in a soft fold of the Cotswold hills, its golden stone cottages reflecting the pale winter sunshine. A small village with a population of just over a thousand, it was the perfect place for Angeline Turney and her husband Richard to raise their children in the safety and peace of the English countryside. The family had relocated from London in the early spring and it took no time at all for them to feel completely at home there.

Minchford fulfilled all their hopes and dreams. The primary school was small with just 66 children and Daniel, seven and Ella, nine were both eagerly welcomed. Angeline felt it was just perfect for them, not so large that they would feel swamped but big enough to give them plenty of friends nearby.

The children had taken the move well and had happily settled into village life. Ella had instantly made friends with three girls of her own age and during the summer they had played at each others' houses and in the small park by the village green.

Daniel was quieter and more introverted than Ella. He enjoyed playing by himself and Angeline had made an extra effort to invite other boys of his age over in the hope that he would make some friends.

Halloween was approaching and both Angeline's children were particularly excited as it was the first time they would be allowed to go trick or treating. Angeline hadn't considered it safe enough to take her children to strangers' houses in London.

After school one day Daniel and his new friend Joe were playing with Dan's train set.

'My mum's going to carve out a pumpkin,' Joe said, 'and there's going to be a candle in the middle and she's putting it in the window to scare everyone on Halloween.'

'Oh I don't think she's doing it to scare people Joe,' said Angeline, 'it's probably to show other children that if they come to your door, there will be goodies for them. Not everyone welcomes children at Halloween, especially old people. Some of them are too frightened to open their doors so it's a good idea putting a jack o'lantern in the window.'

'Why are they too frightened?' piped up Dan, looking anxious.

'Well... when people get old and live alone, they often don't like to open their doors to strangers.'

'You mean like the smelly old man in the Mill Keeper's cottage?' said Joe.

Chilled to the Bone

'Joe, that's very rude! I hope you don't call him that to his face?'

Joe looked up from the train turntable with huge round eyes, 'Not me – I wouldn't call him anything. No-one talks to him, everyone's scared of him.'

Dan stopped running his carriage along the track and looked up at his mother, frown lines creasing his pale brow.

'Nonsense, I'm sure he's quite harmless. He's probably more scared of you than you are of him Joe! Poor man!'

'No, honest,' Joe continued, 'ask anyone! We just call him the Mill Monster – no-one talks to him!'

Angeline watched Dan swallow hard and turn back to his locomotive, pushing it aimlessly backwards and forwards along the track.

When she took Joe back to his mother after tea, she was concerned enough to mention Joe's description of the old man to her.

'Really Kelly, I feel quite sorry for the chap in the Mill Keeper's cottage. Joe was calling him all sorts of dreadful names.'

Quite right Ang, keep your kids well away from him. He's a perv.'

Angeline smiled, 'And you know this how?'

Kelly grimaced and shrugged. 'It's obvious. He

only comes out at night time, you hardly ever see him in the village. His cottage is a disgrace and the garden looks like an open invitation to fly tippers.'

Angeline had to admit that it was true. The Mill Keeper's Cottage was a ruin beside the Minchford brook, once belonging to the silk mill when it was in operation. The Mill had long since gone.

'Perhaps the cottage could be renovated – it was probably a sweet little place in its heyday,' suggested Angeline.

'Yeah, well now it's not sweet and the Mill Monster isn't either so keep your kids away from him.'

Angeline sighed; it was useless trying to change the children's behaviour when the parents were encouraging it.

'Honestly Richard, I wish you could have seen Dan's little face when Joe was talking about the old man in the Mill Keepers' Cottage. He looked terrified.'

Richard stopped cutting into his steak,

'Don't wrap Dan in cotton wool Angeline. You're only making him more frightened. He's already an anxious child - he needs to man up!'

Her mouth dropped open, 'He's seven years old! He can't 'man up', he's a child and I'd like him to stay that way for a little longer!'

'Nonsense. I think I'll have to take charge of our son; he spends far too much time among women.'

'What you going to do, teach him cage fighting?'

Richard stuck out his chin, 'Well, that's the first sensible thing you've said all evening!'

'What!'

'I've been thinking of enrolling him in Taekwan-Do classes – they do them for children in the village hall.'

'No! Over my dead body!'

The following Friday night, Richard took Dan to his first class. When they got back, the boy said very little and went to his room to get ready for bed.

'So... how did that go then? He didn't have much to say for himself when he came in.' Angeline whispered to Richard.

'You know Dan, it takes him a while to warm up. He just sat and watched for the first twenty minutes. Then the instructor had him trying to kick a dummy.'

'Nice!'

'Oh stop it Angie. It's how they start. Martial arts teaches children much more than how to fight. You'll see, it will do him some good. I don't want my son afraid of everything he comes into contact with.'

'I know darling, I know you don't want him to be like you were when your dad got violent... but you're certainly not your father. Dan's just adjusting to his new surroundings. He'll get more confident, give him time. Mrs Lowestock, his class teacher, is keeping her eye on him at school. He's not being bullied.'

'No... and after a few Taekwan-Do lessons, he won't ever be bullied.'

October 31st was a bright day that turned into a cool crisp evening. Ella had gone to Toyah's house where there was a Halloween party and the little girls were all going Trick or Treating together. Angeline silently wished Toyah's mum the best of luck in charge of a group of very excited nine year old witches, fairies and black cats. But then, Toyah was from New York and Halloween was more of a tradition in her family.

Richard had come home from work early, catching the 4:00 pm train so that he could take Dan Trick or Treating himself. Angeline had wanted nothing to do with it; she felt it was a dreadful custom that encouraged children to make a nuisance of themselves. Richard, she suspected, was trying to re-live his own childhood through Dan. Certainly his father had never taken *him* Trick or Treating.

Angeline had just settled down to watch a documentary on the History Channel when she heard Richard calling.

'Come on Dan, show mum. She'll be terrified of you!'

The family room door opened slowly and just for effect, Richard flicked off the light switch. Slowly Dan's little figure emerged into the room, his torso glowing in the skeleton suit Richard had bought for him.

'Put the light back on Rich!'

When the room was once again illuminated she saw her son's little face, poking out of the tight black suit like an extruded blob of toothpaste.

Despite herself, Angeline smiled. Her son looked nervous and excited at the same time. Holding an orange plastic pumpkin bucket in one hand, Dan held tightly onto his dad with the other. Calling 'bye then' over his shoulder, Richard led his son out into the cold night air.

He was determined to show Dan there was nothing to be frightened of. He hadn't mentioned to Angeline that they would be going by Mill Cottage.

To Richard's surprise and delight when they approached the ramshackle old cottage with its crumbling brick walls and rotten wooden fence around the garden, there were lights burning inside.

'Come on then Dan,' said Richard, 'let's go and see what the Mill Monster's like shall we?'

Dan pulled back on his father's hand, trying to steer him away down the street. 'No Dad, I don't want to go in there!' Dan's small voice rose to a shriek.

Richard bent down and looked his son square in the face, 'Now I don't want to hear this nonsense Daniel, show your dad you're not a coward!'

Dan swallowed hard as tears began pooling in the corners of his eyes; his little lips were clamped tightly together. He was as pale as the moon that briefly emerged from behind a slice of cloud.

Richard pulled him towards the front step, the door – open a crack – showed dusty marmalade light glowing inside the hallway.

'Dad… no…it stinks!' said Dan covering his nose with his free hand.

'Dan that's rude. The owner is probably an old man… he might find it hard to keep himself as clean as we do.'

'Please don't make me go in Dad!'

'We're not going inside Dan!' Having reached the front door Richard called out, 'Hi there, we're just trick or treating!'

A frail voice emanated from the depths of the cottage, 'Oh thank goodness. I'm so glad someone's come, I've had a fall. I'm by the sofa in the front room.' The voice of the mill monster sounded elderly and afraid. Dan hesitated and looked up at his dad for direction.

'Ok, Dan...I'm going inside... you just wait here. Do not move from this spot. I may have to call an ambulance.'

Dan nodded unwilling to let his dad go but not wanting to follow him. He watched as his father disappeared into the orange maw of the house.

After a few minutes Dan was getting cold and scared. 'Dad?' Somewhere in the darkness an owl hooted.

'Dad?' he called again. Trembling, he swallowed hard and stepped over the threshold of the cottage and into the front room.

It was sparsely furnished; just an old sofa losing its stuffing and a brown box television sitting on top of a packing case. A damp, fusty odour permeated the air and Dan wrinkled his nose.

Uncertain what to do next, his first instinct was to run home and get his mum but he remembered his dad saying he was supposed to be a man. Holding his breath he moved cautiously into the hallway and through the passage into the dark scullery in the back of the cottage.

'Dad?' he called again in a thin reedy voice. Dan could hear the sound of running water now, quite loud as he approached the open back door. He stepped out into the neglected garden. Dead weeds and fallen tree branches formed eerie shapes in the gloom. Pallid moonlight shone just enough for him to make out the edge of the mill stream where he stopped.

'There you are, son. Come over here!' his father called.

Dan realised he had been holding his breath and ran towards his dad's voice, relieved. At the water's edge was a small shed, the door slightly ajar.

'You in here Dad?'

He gingerly moved into the shed, setting one foot on the wooden floorboards.

'Dad?' he whispered, his voice cracking.

A cobweb brushed his face; he shuddered and frantically swiped it away.

Dan stepped into the shed, his eyes adjusting to the darkness. Instantly, a stench assaulted his nostrils; the rich iron he recognised from his nosebleeds. Only much, much stronger.

'Dad!' he called but no words came out of his throat.

'Yes son, come on in, your treat's in here.'

© Jennie Dobson 2015

# No Party

Not exactly the most glorious conditions for starting a new life. All the kind helpers had trebled their speed over the last hour, desperate to get home before things turned nasty. Four of them had come and persevered until the last box was up on the third floor, but the idea of a celebratory party had not outlived lunchtime.

Adrenaline had been flying high in the morning, when Tony started a fight about the property rights in duvets and pillows, and when every trip in Pete's fully packed van felt like a battle won. What a triumph to set up new book cases and to start filling the wardrobe. *There, you see, everything is possible.*

When Tina noticed her sister's worried looks for the first time, she laughed them off and called her a sissy, but once the TV was in, she went searching for the weather report. Gale force winds and heavy rainstorms ahead, avoid travelling past 5pm. It wasn't too bad for Pete and his mate who lived just 10 minutes away, in one of the villages, but Tina's sister and her husband had quite a bit of motorway ahead of them.

Hence the hurry, and hence her now sitting on her own, staring at taped boxes by candlelight, as the power supply had miserably failed in the storm's first onslaught. What an anti-climax. All the euphoria had seeped away, and with a flat phone battery, there was little chance of reviving it, either. Oh Elizabeth, the party they would have had. She had always known, hadn't she?

Reading was out of the question, so was further unpacking. Tina found a packet of biscuits and withdrew to her cosily made up bed. She must have dozed off the moment she rested her head, because waking up from an extremely uncomfortable dream, she found her bedroom pitch dark, and in the air there was this sooty scent of a burnt down candle going out on its own. *Ouch, that could have gone wrong.*

Power seemed to be back, though, as across the corridor, the fridge was making gargling sounds. That was all – no more rattling roof tiles, no hissing gusts, and an eerie silence from the street. People must have heeded the warning, this was a Saturday, after all. Night, for sure. But what time? She'd have to find her watch.

There, a crack from the staircase. The neighbours? But no sound of a door, nothing from below. Then a very dark clonk, and a thud with a hint of vibration. Tina pulled the duvet over her chin. It might be just the wood. Wood does these things. It works. A rattling from the kitchen. *Okay, that's what the fridge does when it switches off.* She should just go and turn the light on. But...

That was clearly a creaking stair board. Again? Louder than before. The thump of something heavy put down. Like, right in front of her door? Wasn't there even a plink of keys? Tina held her breath. *It might still be the people downstairs.* Silence now, complete silence. Only her heartbeat throbbing in her ears.

Slowly, very slowly she moved one leg out of her bed. *Gosh, it's freezing cold. In October!* Her naked toes touched the ground. Creak, the creaking was back, from the stairs, or the banister? Impossible to tell whether it was nearer or further away. Silence again. She sat up. It was probably time for some noise of her own, TV, anything to stop listening to that crazy wood.

A footstep, one, a whack of something hard falling, knocking on several stairs, another heavy thud, cracking. *A voice?* Quiet, but with irate intonation. *A visitor after all?* Tina grabbed her cardigan. She found the light switch. *Shite, it doesn't work.* Of course, she had wanted to exchange the light bulbs. There was a lighter in the kitchen. She found it, stopped – no more sounds from the stairs. What? Barefoot, very quietly, she made her way to the flat's front door. Hardly daring to breathe, she turned the key and softly, softly pressed down the door handle. The safety light in the staircase came on automatically. A motion detector. Light switch. The antique metal lamp shone a surprisingly bright light, and gently swinging, it had the banister's shadows skipping about. But there was no one. Tina sat down on her threshold, trying to gather her thoughts. Nothing, no one. And absolute silence at the downstairs neighbours'. She shuddered, shook her head and was about to return inside, when she noticed this large wet stain, one stair flight down, on the opposite wall of the landing. A broken pipe? A leak from the roof? That was all she needed tonight.

Tiptoeing down the icy steps, a sudden pain. Something sharp bit into the ball of her right foot. *Stupid, stupid, stupid.* She sat down again, examined it. But nothing, no cut, no blood, it didn't even hurt when pressing on it. *Oh well. Wretched nerves.* But this scent! It must emanate from that wet patch. A few drops had trickled on the floor. Tina dipped her finger into the tiny puddle and held it under her nose. *No way that was water, fresh or from the drains. It smells like... wine, that is what it is, a fruity white wine.*

A distant memory was tickled, flickered. Summer Sundays down by the river, setting the world right with Elizabeth. Best friends forever.

But then... Such a waste of happiness. No, Elizabeth couldn't come anymore.

© Ingrid Stevens 2015

# The Offering

As he turned off the A38 at Liskeard, Peter Ufton knew it wouldn't be long before the roads would narrow to lanes, the hedges would grow denser and higher, the flow of traffic and signs of habitation less, and he would be approaching the isolated Cornish village of Tregolath.

Forty minutes later a faded sign declared he had reached the sparsely populated village, and he slowed further, winding his car along the single-track road that led him through the small settlement. Yet within moments he had passed through the village, continuing south. With his view obscured by the elevated hedgerow that hugged the narrow lane each side of him, Peter began to wonder if he had missed his turning.

*'Take the next turning on the left,'* his satnav dutifully reminded him. Peter scanned ahead for a break in the wind-trimmed brambles and bushes, and saw, lop-sided and disregarded, a hand painted sign leaning against the bracken.

*'Turn left now,'* the invisible navigator prompted again, and without a second thought Peter obeyed.

The crunch of the tyres on the summer-dried road declared his arrival as twigs and tiny stones popped under the weight of the car wheels. Brown field dust ballooned behind and a few bone-shaking seconds over a cattle-grid brought Peter to a stop outside Menhir Farm House.

With the setting sun lighting up the Cornish valley, the fields surrounding the farmhouse were golden in their glory of a ripe harvest. Still pale blue in the distance, the sky dipped to a deep pinky-orange in the west as the sun made its way onward to another morning. Isolated in this hushed tranquillity the thatched grey farmhouse emanated abandonment. Two blank windows stared from its untouched frontage, the walls desiccated by sun and wind, and the whole place looked as though it would crumble into dust in the next breeze. Partially obscured at the back of the farmhouse stood a dilapidated barn.

From the shelter of his car, Peter was drawn to the crest of the hill behind the farmhouse. A line of foreboding Neolithic standing stones zig-zagged down from the horizon like reptilian vertebrae, the setting sun creating long dark shadows as if each stone could not be separated from its prehistoric ghost. Peter was surprised he had not noticed them before. But such was the wonder of the Cornish countryside. So much of what you think you see, you don't, and so much of what you do is no more than a momentary glimpse through trees and hedgerows of something that is never quite there. A mere blink of an eye and whatever you thought you saw is gone. Such was this moment for Peter. Seeing the stones for the first time, they looked to Peter to have been erected in a straight line. He squinted. In the rapidly changing light, the columns appeared to slowly twist and turn, advancing toward the house. They weren't of course. But just for a moment, for the briefest blink in time, it looked like they did, pushed gradually forward by their extending shadows.

Standing as silent sentinels to an ancient past, each stone loomed 15 feet high and more. Any inscription or adornment had long ago been polished away by centuries of soft Cornish rain and westerly winds. Now they remained, embedded deep in the soil, blind and anonymous custodians of their land.

Glancing again at the eerie columns Peter took a deep breath and clicked open the car door. Simultaneously, the door of the farmhouse opened and a woman stood there, her ill-fitting careworn clothes held in place by a small soiled apron. In her left hand she held a spade. Out of the gloom of the hallway behind her, a large black dog lumbered into view and they stood motionless for a moment, side-by-side, like grotesque conjoined twins. Patiently they waited for Peter to open the car door fully. He hesitated. The woman stepped out into the evening light and leaned the spade on the wall by the door, then slowly began wiping her hands on her apron. Wishing he were heading back up the A38 homeward, Peter quickly glanced at his phone. He was not surprised to see there was still no signal. It had been like that for a while. Grabbing his briefcase from the passenger seat and pushing open the door, Peter Ufton smiled and got out of his car.

'Mrs Trescothic?' he asked, walking toward the woman he assumed was his client.

'Tha's me,' she replied, and the dog woofed in a quietly menacing way.

'*Diwettha*,' the woman urged the dog softly, as she switched effortlessly to her native Cornish and spoke just loud enough for the dog to hear. The dog stayed still.

Peter's instinct was to run, to get away, back into the car and go. He did not like the dog. He did not like the woman much either. Instead, he extended his hand with a counterfeit confidence he hoped she would not detect.

'I'm...'

'I know who you are. Mr Ufton. The Picture Man,' replied Mrs Trescothic softly.

'Ah... yes... that's right. Pleased to meet you.' Peter felt and sounded awkward.

'Please, come in,' she said. 'Nice to 'ave a bit of

company. I don't get many visitors out 'ere.' Mrs Trescothic smiled a rotten-toothed smile at Peter and his stomach tightened. Her pale blue eyes, ugly rheumy orbs in a small, closed face, studied him closely. Stepping closer to the house the embossed initials on Peter's briefcase caught the orange sunlight and reflected it across the dog's face in a flash. Both dog and owner blinked. Mrs Trescothic peered at the letters LSA.

'London Society of Art,' stated Peter, by way of explanation when he saw her looking at his briefcase.

'Well, I suppose you would be, otherwise you wouldn't be 'ere. Fancy a cold drink Mr Ufton? You looks 'ot,' she said, in her lilting Cornish brogue, and without waiting for an answer she turned into the gloom of the farmhouse.

'Oh no, I'm fine thank you. Not long had one,' Peter lied. He followed her into the house aware that the dog seemed to hold back, waiting for the slightest of chances, the merest opportunity - or so it seemed to Peter - to bite him. Then, without instruction and just a footstep behind, the dog followed him in.

Mrs Trescothic shuffled deeper into the gloom of the house and once inside, Peter tried not to stare. It was clear that Mrs Trescothic was a hoarder. The house was stuffed full with the worst sort of bric-a-brac. Piled high each side of the low-ceilinged dingy hallway were yellowed newspapers and old books, empty yoghurt cartons, bits of broken tools and unidentifiable parts of motors and engines, and what could have been fragments of mobile phone cases or computer parts. Several pairs of men's shoes sat abandoned in a pile, a walking stick lying across them. The air in the house smelled stale and cloying, and Peter's eyes watered.

'Just in 'ere,' said Mrs Trescothic, and he edged his way behind her along the narrow pathway and into a large room.

A wide inglenook fireplace dominated the far end and everywhere was more tat and junk. Black sooty residue clung to the back wall behind the fire and a bulky pile of old cold ash littered the tiles beneath the log grate. Peter stared. It looked like the entrance to a derelict mausoleum.

Above this enormous fireplace hung a portrait. It wasn't the fabled piece of artwork he had come to see, but it was unnervingly arresting all the same.

'Tha's my dear departed,' Mrs Trescothic said, offering him a glass of murky liquid from a tray balanced on a pile of dusty books. 'Lem'n squash,' she smiled. Peter felt a lump in this throat as he returned her smile, his eyes fixed on the rotten stumps of her teeth. 'I always 'as some made up ready, for when it get's 'ot,' she said. 'Drink up.'

'Thank... you,' said Peter.

He toyed with the grubby glass for as long as he could; to his horror he noticed it hadn't been washed. Soon warming from the heat of his hand, what he assumed to be flecks of lemon began to sink to the bottom of the glass forming thin grey sediment. He felt Mrs Trescothic's eyes on him.

'Mr Trescothic?' said Peter, nodding towards the portrait.

'Ah. Tha's so. Felix Trescothic. Known as Moses,' she answered.

'Oh. A Jewish connection?' he asked.

'Oh no!' she said. 'On account that 'e could play th' piano.'

Peter frowned. 'I don't see…'

'*Moses Mendelssohn*, father of *Felix*. Th' composer,' explained Mrs Trescothic. Peter didn't reply.

'Drink up,' said Mrs Trescothic again. 'You look 'ot.'

Peter didn't want to. He didn't want to at all, but there was something in the keenness of her eyes that made him oblige her. He desperately wanted to see the painting she purported to own - *a lost Rembrandt*. If it was true, and he could convince her to sell, his commission would see him healthily into retirement.

Feeling her pale eyes upon him, Peter capitulated and sipped sagaciously at the drink, despite his better judgement.

If it took drinking a glass of horrid homemade lemonade to get her to hand over the painting, he would. It was hardly much to ask. Steeling his nerves, he opened his mouth and swallowed the drink as fast as he could, swiftly handing her back the dirty glass. Mrs Trescothic smiled again.

'Take a seat,' she said calmly.

Peter rubbed his forehead and looked around. There was hardly a space for him to perch, let alone sit. Everywhere was dirty and grime-laden, and he was getting very, very hot. But he had to keep calm - it didn't seem inconceivable that there could be a picture - probably worth millions - hidden amongst all this rubbish. He had heard stranger stories.

'The... er...picture then, Mrs Trescothic. The one you wanted me to value. Can I see it?'

Peter rubbed his eyes and the bridge of his nose. He took a deep breath.

'I...I'm sorry, I don't feel...'

'I know you don't chap, I know you don't,' said Mrs Trescothic, almost as a matter of course. 'Here, sit down,' she said, and pressed him into a chair he didn't realise was behind him. Peter fell

## Chilled to the Bone

heavily onto the grubby cushion, his arms hanging loosely over each side of the chair. His body was so heavy. He tried to lift his head, to speak, but the drug surging through him rendered him helpless. With panic rising like a hungry flame through paper, Peter rasped with horror as the dog padded softly over to him and sat down.

'*No...please...n...,*' he managed to whisper, but his paralysis was complete.

The dog began to lick his fingers.

Mrs Trescothic drew her shrivelled face close and her small eyes looked coldly into his. Pressing her bony fingers on his neck she checked Peter's slackening pulse.

'*What did you...*' Peter said weakly, his final words failing in his throat.

Peter heard his heart pounding in his head, every heartbeat like the clang of a blacksmith's hammer on its anvil, gently slowing to almost a stand-still. But not quite.

The old woman moved swiftly and expertly, deftly and silently, making sure that Peter Ufton was alive for nearly all of it. It was the way she had always done it.

Accompanied by her dog, Mrs Trescothic was digging, unhurriedly, in her well-tended vegetable patch when the police called by a few days later.

They were making enquiries.

'No, I've not seen no-one,' she said to them, resting to lean her aged body on her equally aged spade. Pausing from gnawing a large white bone, the dog looked intently at the enquiring officer, holding his gaze. Sticky white foam dribbled from its teeth and fell slowly onto the dusty ground. The officer got back into the police car.

'Well, thank you for your time. Let us know if you do,' he said. 'Looks like you'll have a good harvest,' he continued from the open window, nodding toward the verdant vegetation.

"S'been a good summer,' she replied.

The officers bid her goodbye and turned the car back toward the sandy lane that led away from the farmhouse. The dog resumed gnawing.

She wiped her hands on her grubby apron and listened as the car rumbled over the disused cattle grid and away into the distance.

Returning to her digging, the perpetual westerly breeze blew very gently across the blind faces of the silent standing stones.

© Jacci Gooding 2015

# Face to Face

'Change your clothes, child,' Gran says. Her voice is one of those serious ones. 'Wear something to cover your arms. And take this soft blanket to put round your shoulders. The November night-air is cold.'

Gran lives in a small village on the edge of a tropical rain forest, which gives me a cosy feeling, because I live in the city. Tonight is chilly though. I pull a soft jersey top over my head, and slip on some trousers. She's looking down at me and I'm looking up thinking *I love you Gran*. She's not that old or wrinkled for a grandmother. This evening she has a radiant look of yellow around her, and her green eyes are sparkling as if she's excited. I am too. We're going on a night-time adventure. Gran gives me anything I want, and she's good at stories, and her food is the best ever, which is why I like coming to stay. It keeps her company too. She lives on her own, but she's scared of nothing. The best thing about her is that she tells me strange stories.

'It's All Saints night,' she says. 'The night when lost souls are supposed to find their way to heaven.' I stare at her and shiver a little because I feel a strange story coming. 'Come now Lilly, hurry. Bring the bag with the candles and matches. We've to go and light the family graves.'

'Whose graves?' I asked. 'We buried Tabby cat in my back garden at home.'

'People, Lilly. Not cats or dogs, nor cows or goats.'

'Chickens?' I add. 'What about them? Don't they have souls?'

'Of course not!' She looks at me like I'm being silly. 'People Lilly, people. Those whose souls are out there unable to find rest.'

'But in the dark?' I ask. 'Can't they just close their eyes and go back to sleep?'

'I expect they will, after we've gone. But if it's true that they are lost, we may as well help them. We wouldn't want them to be lost in the forest forever now, would we?' Besides, it's the night after Halloween, so we should help them. I don't care much for all that Halloween sorcery either. It's a lot of nonsense. We'll go and light the candles, just in case. You never know.'

'Halloween is fun. Yesterday my friends and I had a lot of fun being witches on broomsticks, and eating cakes, and sweets.'

'Your mother lets you go out on Halloween by yourselves? In the city?' Gran isn't sounding too happy so I don't answer. 'Listen Lilly, I want to tell you something important. We're going to the cemetery which is close to the forest. So I want you to keep close. Do you hear me? Keep close. This is not the city with bright-glaring-lights everywhere. You mustn't wander away from me, will you?'

'The cemetery?' I shriek. 'In the forest? We're going to the forest? But it's nearly dark Gran. We'll never find our way out. We'll be lost forever.'

'Not if you stay close, Lilly. You're a big girl. When I was seven I was cooking a whole meal for my family. I promise we won't get lost.'

Gran pulls the blanket over my shoulders. 'You take the bag with the candles,' she says. 'The quicker we go, the quicker we'll get back.'

She picks up a machete from under the stairs and we go out. I feel safe snuggled under my warm blanket and Gran carrying a machete. We leave the house and begin to walk. The moon is hiding behind a cloud just like me behind my blanket.

'There are things you town folk need to know when you come down to the Caribbean countryside. It's not all about sandy beaches and swimming in the sea, you know. Things happen. Things you don't know about. Have you ever been lost?'

It's almost dark, and the dogs have stopped barking. 'No-o-o,' I begin to shiver.

'So let's keep it that way. We don't know who or

what's out there, apart from lost souls.'

I walk closer to Gran, almost touching her skirt as it swishes in the silent night. Fireflies dart here and there in front of us but not for long. It's as if they too are afraid. People are walking behind us, murmuring. Some in front of us too, but no one is talking loud enough for me to hear what they're saying. I wish they would slow down so we could catch up with them. I'd prefer we were all together. An owl hoots and flies past, which makes me jump, and grab Gran's skirt.

'Owls are just night birds,' she says. 'Their eyes can't adjust to daylight.'

'Is that because they open them too wide?'

'Maybe,' Gran whispers.

A girl in front of us is crying, and we both walk faster to catch up as they slow down. A woman and two children.'

'I want to see Papa,' the girl in front cries. 'I want my Papa.' She's no more than four.

'That's Minah,' Gran whispers. 'Paulette's daughter. Her husband died in an accident at work last week. A tree fell on him. Killed him almost at once. We buried him in the cemetery right here.'

I remember the name Paulette. And I remember the little girl from last year when I visited Gran. She was too small to play with me. Couldn't catch a ball or even play hopscotch. I didn't know her father had died though. I expect Gran would have told me later. Hearing Minah cry like that makes me really sad. It makes me think of my own Dad. Suddenly I'm scared about going to the cemetery.

'Gran, can we turn back?' I ask. 'I don't feel I want to go there anymore.'

'After we light the candle on my mother's grave, and your great uncle's.'

'Are they still lost? Haven't they found their way to heaven or Afghanistan yet?'

'Afghanistan? Where did you get that from?'

'Dad,' I say. 'He said Afghanistan was hell on earth.'

A rush of wind blows past. 'I'm freezing Gran.' I pull the blanket tight around my neck. Just then behind a clump of trees, I spot the cemetery lit up, glittering with flickering lights. The wind is blowing cold on my cheeks and neck and people move around the lights, casting shadows on the ground and across the grave stones. The murmuring, and moaning, and crying everywhere makes my stomach shake inside me. Gran takes hold of my hand tight, and we march towards the lights between the grave stones, and suddenly a horrible thought of walking on the dead people under the ground makes me want to jump up in the air and run home. I worry a skeleton will grab my feet and twist and break them. Gran squeezes my wrist tight as we move quickly now through the men, women and children sitting on the grass, standing around, staring and drinking beer and cola from bottles.

Gran stops and asks me to hand her the candles, and I take them out of the bag and hand them to her one by one. She sticks them into the ground and asks me for the box of matches and I hand her that too. Soon my great grandma's grave is lit like a Christmas tree, and I see shapes floating around in the dark. I have no idea what they are, but we move along and do the same on my great uncle's grave. Then another little one. I'm starting to hate it here, and desperate to go home so I don't ask any more questions. We stand and watch our candles burn. We watch other people's candles burn too, and I count them. Then I say I'm really tired now.

'Time we left then,' she says, and we begin to walk.

The woods seem alive, with shadows and light coming from the cemetery and a big moon. My teeth chatter so I don't talk any more. Gran starts talking to people who have the same idea about leaving. I keep my eye on Gran's flowered dress, but then I think I am lagging behind, because she seems far away. I try to speed up but my legs are tired. The flowered dress disappears. I spot it again, and keep my eyes on it, barely looking where I'm going. I turn left.

An owl floats past me. I know because I feel the cold rush of air bat past my face. Suddenly tall trees surround me, and the dress has disappeared. I'm all alone. Gran has gone. I scream but there's no sound. I don't know where I am. I want my Mummy.

I'm tired. It feels as if I've been asleep for hours and have just woken up. I open my eyes wide like an owl and find I'm looking at a reflection of myself right in front of me. But it's a baby. I'm surrounded by tall trees that look like an umbrella at the top in the sky. And that thing in front of me is a black mirror. I'm staring myself in the face. I check to see if it's me. Same hair, same eyes, same height, same age. Just like me from head to... Oh! My feet are broken and turned backwards.

'Lilly? Come,' she speaks like a baby. 'Follow me. We need to go home.' But the baby sounds like a man. The voice is deep at the end. I'm not sure of anything now, and I freeze. My feet are like lumps of iron. The baby takes my hand and pulls me hard towards it. Or is it towards me? I shiver and walk, scared of not doing as it says. I have no choice, so I watch myself walking backwards.

'Have I broken my feet?' I managed to ask as politely as I could. But then she pulls me and I am running. Faster and faster until I feel my feet leave the ground and I'm flying through the trees, between the branches and through the leaves, in and out, and up and down. What's happening? Is this the new me? Am I dead? Is my spirit, some ghost of me returning here and there, flying and flitting? I'm lost. I know I am lost, but how, and why? What happened?

The baby's voice is suddenly not a baby's any more. It is deep, and grunting more like a pig. 'Haha! Haha! Lilly! Lilly my lovely Lilly! Silly Lilly! Silly Lilly lost her Milly!'

'Put me down!' I scream. 'Put me down! Graaaaaannnnn!'

I feel myself falling, falling, falling, and then I land with such a thump that I bounce back up again and then down. The trees shake and echoes of my screams fly through the village. Hundreds of footsteps begin running through the forest, getting closer and closer. Faces peer over me. Gran and a whole load of people arrive and find me lying flat on my back staring shocked into the dark sky.

'Oh, it found her,' someone says. But it's not Gran who speaks. Gran just stares at me. She stoops down and scoops me up in her arms.

'That was the *duenne*, sweety. The evil *duenne* that lives in the forest. Someone must have called out your names, yours and your sister's. It's probably been looking for her until it found you. You must have confused him. Or she might have found you first, before he found you both. Good job you screamed. Or he would have taken you far away. Doesn't bear thinking. Maybe I should have not brought you out. I should have known.'

'That small grave, Gran. Whose was that? Was it hers? I never knew I had a sister.'

'She was taken at birth dear. Your identical twin, Milly.'

© Marilyn Rodwell 2015

# The Challenge

The night was dark and stormy. There was a full moon up there somewhere but the cloud cover was so thick not so much as a glimmer of it penetrated. But the wind howled and the girl pulled her navy woolly hat further down over her ears and was glad of the matching scarf that hid most of her face. It had rained heavily during the day but thankfully that had stopped a couple of hours ago. Perfect, she thought, as she quickly walked the deserted pavements, glad of the all encompassing darkness.

Unfortunately, the uneven pavements harboured numerous puddles which she didn't even try to sidestep – so focused as she was on the job in hand. She paid no attention to the discomfort of her sodden footwear. She also kept as far away as possible from the occasional muted streetlamp ensuring she wouldn't be spotted by anyone daft enough to be out on a night like this. She wasn't wearing gloves as they would be a hindrance but kept her hands in the pockets of her school mac. She clasped her right hand round the small but powerful torch her grandfather had given her. She had no intention of using it – she wasn't afraid of the dark. No, it was merely a talisman, a reminder of the old man to give her the courage to see this night through.

She came to the lychgate that marked the entrance to the small Saxon church. Resting her hand lightly on the gate she debated her choices. The path through the churchyard would be quicker and safer but they would be watching and waiting for her by that route and she knew the gate's hinges had probably not been oiled in the last 50 years. The noise from them alone would alert them to her presence.

She thought of her grandfather. 'Gird your loins and soldier on', he would say. He had an odd saying for every occasion it seemed. Some she understood, others he would explain and yet others he merely tapped her forehead with his finger and urged her to 'use your noddle'.

She loved her grandfather and spent as much time as possible with him. He didn't judge her — not like her parents. He accepted her for what she was — an 11 year old girl who was small enough to pass for an eight or nine year old. She had overheard her parents arguing once. Her father had wanted a strapping son but apparently her mother had had such a hard labour when giving birth to her, well she had no intention of going through that again, thank you very much!

No, she thought, if she was to succeed it had to

be the hard way so mentally girding her loins she soldiered on except now she counted every step. 'One, two' splish, 'three, four' splosh. She continued until she had counted 47. Putting her hand out to the side she felt the iron railing that surrounded the property that bordered the churchyard. More importantly she found the gap created by a missing spar. She had located it when she recced the area on her way home from school two days ago. Stooping down she put one foot through the gap and wriggled the rest of her body through, for once being glad of her slight stature. Once inside she stayed stooped and gingerly probed the long wet grass until her hand closed on the iron bar that had once kept people on the outside. She pulled it out of the grass and stood up, hefting it in her hand to test its weight. She would have preferred Excaliber but as her grandfather was always telling her, 'don't wish for what you don't have but make the most of what is to hand'. The iron bar would definitely suit her purpose and being predominantly black and rust she had no fear that a stray moonbeam might be reflected in it.

She started down the narrow path that had been trodden by countless others before her, careful to avoid the thick shrubbery. She was especially careful around the thick brambles that seemed to cover everything. Wet shoes and socks she could conceal but a torn new school mac – well, the repercussions to that didn't bear thinking about.

A wet furry animal ran across her foot. She instinctively jumped back a step and clasped her free hand to her mouth to stifle a cry of alarm. 'Get a grip, you wuss' she silently admonished herself. It was only a nocturnal animal out looking for a meal. Nothing to be frightened of, nothing - evil.

Her parents had gone to great lengths to shelter her against the world and all its evils. They were, however, unaware that she paid avid attention to the 6 o'clock news on the TV whilst appearing to be studiously concentrating on her homework. When possible she would also filch yesterday's newspaper from the recycling bin and surreptitiously sneak it up to her room where she devoured its contents. Even the sports pages held evidence of corruption and disgusting behaviour. Yes, she was no stranger to evil. Her grandfather had also schooled her. 'Better to be aware of what's out there' he would say. 'No point in being led up the garden path, like a lamb to the slaughter'.

Her heart was still beating ten to the dozen so she took a big breath and let it out slowly whilst counting down from ten to zero. Satisfied that her heart rate was back to normal she continued down the path, going even slower now as the shrubbery gave way to trees and saplings.

She smelt him before she saw him. Her night vision was as good as any cat and she scanned the area in front of her, easily spotting the sentinel. His back was towards her, leaning against a tree whilst smoking a cigarette. She smiled to herself and continued on ever more slowly putting one foot in front of the other, rather like a tightrope walker feeling his way, not putting her weight down until she was sure of her footing. When she was only a few feet away she raised the iron bar and brought it smartly down on his shoulder. 'You're dead' she hissed through clenched teeth. He turned towards her, surprise and horror on his face but as he mumbled an expletive he slowly crumpled to the sodden earth.

She gingerly stepped over him steeling herself from looking back. She had a fleeting memory of a much younger self taking a leaping jump onto her bed at night in case a bogeyman lurked under it. She half expected a hand to slither along the ground and grab her ankle. She realised she was holding her breath and let it out slowly before moving forward.

She heard singing, or was it chanting, she wasn't quite sure so she pushed her hat back up over her ears in order to hear better. But then suddenly there was light before her. She edged towards the perimeter of a clearing, staying a few feet inside the tree-line.

Before her she saw a huge bonfire with a crowd of people, some in hideous masks, cavorting around it. Her eyes were drawn to a tall figure standing to one side. He was head and shoulders taller than anyone else there and had long horns protruding from his forehead. His floor length scarlet cape billowed in the gentle breeze. Had the wind dropped while she had been in the wood or did it not dare to penetrate this unhallowed ground? She was not sure. The worst feature though was his eyes. They were large and glassy and in the reflected light from the bonfire they burned like red hot coals.

She shivered, but undeterred reminded herself of the task before her. She wouldn't get a second chance. She peeped her head out and took a quick look left and right. Sure enough, two more sentinels stood on the periphery some 20 yards on either side. She might be small but, she reminded herself, she was faster than most boys her age.

Taking a deep breath she sprinted forward. Shouts went up behind her but she ignored them and carried on, arms and legs pumping, adrenalin coursing through her body. Eyes fixed firmly on the beast she made a beeline for her target. Fortunately there was so much noise from the revellers no-one heard her pursuers' shouts. When she was only a few paces away she raised the iron bar above her head in a two-handed grip. Leaping as high as she could she took an almighty swing and brought the bar down on the side of its head which flew from its body, landing with a sickening thud on the wet ground before rolling to a stop a few yards away, the glassy eyes looking accusingly up at her.

Undaunted she dropped the bar and punched the air with a triumphant cry. Suddenly exhausted she bent double, grabbing her knees whilst trying to get more air into her spent lungs.

The two sentinels finally caught up to her and she fearlessly turned to face them. 'Bloody hell, it's a first former' one cried, 'and a girl at that!' 'We're never going to live this down' complained the other. Disgusted with their performance they turned and trudged back to their places of concealment.

A woman stepped from the crowd and lovingly picked up the decapitated head which she then forced back on to a spike which protruded from between the beast's shoulder blades. 'Well done!' she cried. Then, looking at the girl, 'is that you Monica?'

Monica removed her woolly hat and shook out her golden curls. 'Yes, Miss Stevenson' she replied.

'Congratulations, you're the first to best Old Nick tonight and I do think you are the only first former in the school's history to do so. Come and get a hot drink' she added, guiding Monica over to a long trestle table. She handed her a steaming plastic cup of red liquid which looked remarkably like blood. Monica took a tentative sip and wrinkled her nose. Strawberry! - she should have guessed.

Her friend Grace spied her. 'Mo, what are you doing here? I thought your parents forbade you to come tonight, pagan rituals and all that'. Monica just shrugged. Her friend laughed. 'How on earth are you ever going to get back home without being caught out?'

The girl thought about the old man and all that he had taught her. 'Piece of cake' she replied.

© Dianne Lee 2015

# Diamorphine

They would gather at night, the same six, taking up their positions around my bed. The night Sister spoke about my experience politely but with obvious exasperation. 'I tell you, there's nothing there, Mr Gulliver. It's quite normal, I assure you. Now! Just ignore them. Close your eyes. And go back to sleep.'

Closed or open, it made no difference; they still gathered, too distinct and solid to be a figment of my imagination. Naturally, I looked for rational explanations: hospital equipment taking on humanoid shapes cast by the light of the nurses' station, reflections, a repetitive dream, images made by a human prankster.

It seemed to bemuse my gathered friends who gazed upon me in kindly, but somewhat sad, pity. Or, at least, one of them did, an imposing fellow dressed in tunic and breeches who seemed to speak for them all. Not by word of mouth, you understand, but more by the subtlest and yet easily decipherable changes of expression and mood.

I began to take more notice of the others. At the foot of my bed were two nurses, though not of a modern era. Behind them, on the periphery of things, lingered a tall figure in black. Next, at my side, knelt a girl no, not a girl, more a young woman, bent over my bed with her face buried in my blanket. That left the last of the six, the most unobtrusive of them all, sitting slightly behind me, so that all I could see of him was his knees and the quality of his suit. The texture and style of its cloth reminded me of someone. Someone I knew, a distinguished figure who I couldn't for the life of me place.

I could stand it no longer and turned back to the one in breeches, who by now I had taken to be their leader. 'What is it you want? I mean – tell me! What d'you want!'

He moved closer. As kindly as he had always been, he made it clear he wished me to know who he was, and drew attention to his chest. In it, set like rubies, were a number of raw wounds.

I searched through history, but could think of only one possible name. 'Rasputin? Is that it? You're Rasputin?'

Such was the air of disappointment emanating from the fellow, I searched on. But it was no use. I could think of no-one. It was an impossible task – impossible! Then he raised a finger, the first tangible sign of physical communication, a gesture I readily understood. I was to be patient and watch.

He undid the lower buttons on his tunic and

held it apart. Unlike all the other wounds, the one he revealed still oozed blood. But I was no further forward and shook my head. 'I'm sorry, I just – I can't think. I'm sorry!'

The girl, woman – whatever she was – wept silently on, face buried. The two nurses stood as though in attendance, waiting for some command. The figure in black also waited, as detached as ever, looking in at me through a window I knew for a fact wasn't there. There was no window. It did not exist.

Up came that finger, cautioning me once more, bidding me wait. To my astonishment, the arm supporting the in-hospital entertainment services swung round, bringing with it a lighted screen. Music sounded…a theme tune I vaguely recognized. With it, came footsteps, ringing hollow and eerily down what appeared to be a medieval street. I suggested Jerusalem, more in hope than belief. 'Damascus?'

I was way off the mark, not even close. Deflated, I eyed the two nurses. Of different faiths, it struck me, though up until that point I had had no reason to think it. It just seemed the case, almost a certainty, that one was Christian the other Moslem.

The Crimea! Now, I was getting somewhere. The Crimea was about the only time the two might have come into contact. Mid to late nineteenth century, I calculated, certainly no earlier and most unlikely any later.

Clearly sensing my excitement, my friend swung the television screen back in front of me. Up came the same scene, the same music, the same hollow footsteps leading … 'Alec d'Urberville! You're Alec d'Urberville. And this, this must be Tess!'

I placed my hand upon the young woman's head, lightly, barely touching her hair. The head beneath moved. "Yes", it seemed to be saying. "Yes! Yes! Yes!"

Such was her agony I could do no other than administer what comfort came to mind, a stroking, not necessarily of hair, but something that felt more like a ball of shredded paper.

My fingers curled and dug into my palm. Tess and Alec d'Urberville. But this couldn't be. Tess and Alec d'Urberville were fictional characters. But then, was it not feasible that Hardy had based his story on a real event – yes, quite feasible.

I squeezed my eyes shut and breathed through my open mouth, helping my new heart settle and, given time, beat more evenly.

Only the figure in black acted less than impressed, though no feature penetrated that window of his, the one I kept reminding myself did not exist, that with the blink of an eye was no more. It had gone, the fellow now standing on the inside, fleshless, all bone it seemed. Yet there was no clue to any of it. Nothing showed from beneath his black garb.

Nothing...

Again, I closed my eyes and did as the night Sister had demanded. I tried to sleep. These were the hours I dreaded, that long haul sandwiched between the Horlicks and the far-off chinking of crockery, sometimes imagined, sometimes not.

I awoke sweating, my foot clamped. There was a sensation of cutting, a methodical separation of toe from toe. I could feel the blood oozing from each and every stroke of the scalpel. I could see them, the two nurses, huddled over me at the foot of my bed.

'Mr Gulliver! Mr Gulliver, you must stay calm. Please, for the sake of the other patients, if nothing else!'

I admit that I wanted to run, but stood no chance, not surrounded as I was and sprouting more tubes and wires than Andy Pandy had strings. I wanted the police. I knew my rights, but Sister took no notice. She straightened my pillows, stuck a thermometer in my ear and replaced the clip I had dislodged from my finger, bringing immediate calm to the ward and an end to that infernal bleeping. Lastly, she inserted the oxygen supply back into my nostrils, 'You're doing yourself no favours, Mr Gulliver. BP sky-high. Oxygen down to eighty-one. If this goes on, we're going to have to sedate you. D'you understand?'

Appearing to want neither reply nor reaction, she stood with her fingers pressed to the pulse in my wrist, monitoring the reading, not letting go for some considerable time. 'Now, keep your oxygen supply in,' she said, laying my wrist to rest. 'Nobody's doing any cutting. There's nobody there. Go back to sleep.'

I did as she ordered, took in the oxygen, closed my eyes and lay still, ignoring the workings of the two nurses as they snipped and trimmed their way up my leg.

There it was, held up for all to see – a vein. But it had already been taken, I reminded myself. It was an illusion. I was doing well. I was perfectly calm, even when a section of bone was held up for my inspection, the sort one might have thrown to a dog. Even then, I wasn't fazed. Oh yes, I say that, but my new heart let me know it was there, thumping for release from inside its cage. But I stayed calm – I did!

I did, I did…

The two nurses rose as one, their work apparently done, but there was no gap in my leg, no blood, no section of missing bone. What was more, I could waggle my toes.

Something had changed, though. Clearly, the nurses had finished their work: on the other hand, the work was clearly not finished. I sensed it: a mood: an air of anticipation, all eyes concentrating on the distinguished gentleman sitting in my bedside chair.

It was my surgeon. No, my childhood GP – a cross between the two! Taking over from where the nurses had left off, he made use of what I can only describe as tongs, followed by a scalpel, drawn across my shoulder and into my neck. But no further, I vowed, pushing away the instruments.

No more ... please.

No more...

Alec d'Urberville laid a pistol on my chest, long barrelled and evil. A diversionary tactic, some devilish trick, no doubt, and it all began to make sense. They were after my heart. They wanted my new heart, but they weren't going to get it. I grappled with hands as solid and real as my own. Even though the weight of the pistol made it difficult to breathe, and regardless of the damage I might have done to myself, I pushed and grabbed at everything.

Against all the odds, I won the day. Oh, I had

won all right. By all the Saints, I had won; only to find myself staring into the perfect round of a pistol barrel. 'Go on, then! Shoot why don't you? Shoot!'

Victory was mine. The pistol faded from view. Alec d'Urberville disappeared. They all disappeared. All, that was, with the exception of the one in black.

Beyond him, stood a horse and carriage, again all black; everything black save for the contrasting beauty of the wheel spokes, the colour and reassuring warmth of polished beech. Civilly, he opened the door and invited me to enter, beckoning with one long, crooked, skeletal finger.

© David Nelmes 2015

# For Better for Worse

As long as I'd known him he'd wanted this house. Coveted it, almost, so that now that we had it, it had to be perfect. Picture perfect. The noise of it all was driving me crazy. A sudden crash made me look to the ceiling. A man's face appeared from the loft.

'So sorry, love, it was only my toolbox. I nearly dropped it through the joists. Would've been a pain, if that had happened.' Then he beckoned. 'Can you come up here for a moment, pet?'

I wasn't that fond of climbing ladders, but nor was I fond of looking a fool, so I did what he asked and climbed the ladder. The man turned around, he was clutching a bag. A huge plastic bag. 'I think this is yours, love.'

I knew when I saw it, it definitely wasn't. But I also knew he wanted shut, so I carefully carried it back down the ladder, thinking as I did so, how weightless it seemed. Then I ripped it open, quick as a flash. Inside was a dress, an old wedding dress.

I unwrapped the contents, piece by piece, the dress, a veil, some pieces of ribbon, even a horseshoe with wedding cake on. The whole package was total nostalgia. How could the woman have left me all this? Later that day, I went round to her house.

We hadn't been in our home for long. The previous owner, the mildest of women, had been happy for me to have her address. In case you have any questions, she said.

Well, I did have questions, a lot of questions, but not about plumbing or central heating. I handed the woman the plastic bag. 'This is yours, I presume?' Waited for her to thank me, happily. She visibly flinched.

'Oh no,' she said. 'It's not my dress. It belonged to my husband, David's, first wife.'

I knew when she said it, what would happen to the thing. The dress would be given away to charity, dumped in the dirty doorway of a shop, she wouldn't be able to bear keeping it, even overnight. The rain would come down and leak through the plastic I'd carelessly torn, just hours before. The dress would be ruined, ripped, destroyed, it was gorgeous, lovely, layers of lace. I couldn't bear to think of its end.

'If you don't want the dress,' I said, hesitant, 'I could give it to a friend at the local theatre. They're always looking for clothes for costumes. I'm sure they'd be grateful, really grateful.' The woman smiled.

'Why, of course you can have it,' she said, nodding. 'Only please don't tell them where it came from.'

Bridget Malansie, for that was her name, didn't think, I'm sure, that I needed advice, about heating, the drains or the day for recycling, or any other thing connected with the house. I'm sure she'd realised, right from the start, that I was just nosey, which was why I suggested we went for a coffee. I wanted to know more about David's first wife. It took a little while to get the story.

'She was murdered, you know, that's why I didn't want the dress in the house.'

'Murdered?' I said. I was so surprised I spilt my tea. 'That must have been awful for your husband.' But the woman looked smug.

'Oh, no, Belinda, you've got it all wrong. My husband and her weren't together by then. They'd already gone their separate ways. He was shocked of course, but that was all.'

'Oh, right,' I said, thinking, all the same, it must have been a bad shock.

'The woman was a bit of a tart, you see. David was sure she had a lover; he told me he could never find proof, but he said he could smell him, something on her, after she'd seen him, tobacco, aftershave, something distinctive. I never believed him at the time.'

Her eyes glazed over, slipped back to the past.

Then her gaze sharpened.

'I thought it was all an excuse to meet me, have an affair. But, now I believe him, though we still don't *know*. The woman must have been really easy. He finally divorced her, married me instead.' She looked triumphant.

I grinned at my newly found confidante.

'So who murdered her in the end? I'm assuming it wasn't your husband, of course.' I laughed as I said it, I didn't want to offend Bridget. But she seemed to take my words seriously.

'No, of course it wasn't, but nobody knows who killed Samantha, they never found out who the culprit was. At least her and David had split up by then.'

*And she wasn't murdered in my house*, I said to myself, but of course, not out loud. Imagining Samantha, David's first wife, murdered in my beautiful home. Did that mean I thought he'd done it?

After that day we were almost an item, Bridget and I, we met up frequently, usually over coffee, to talk about children (she had two), careers for women ('wrong,' she said, 'marriage is the perfect career for a woman'), clothes and cupcakes (hers were lovely – the cupcakes I mean). But we always, eventually, got round to the murder.

'Poor little Samantha Malansie, no-one ever wanted her.' This was Bridget.

*Apart from your husband and a lover,* I said to myself. 'You've changed your tune,' I told her, mildly. We were trying out somewhere new for coffee, I didn't much like it. Bridget looked guilty.

'I was thinking about how I'd called her a trollop, I wasn't being kind, I guess I was jealous. She always looked lovely, so pretty, attractive, *and* she was clever, the woman had it all, whereas I...' she trailed off, shrugged her shoulders.

'I'd known Samantha before she was married, not known to speak to, but just at a distance, we were at the same college, we did the same course. We were chalk and cheese, Samantha and I, we could never have been friends.' She stared at her plate and lapsed into silence.

I could see what she meant, Bridget looked smart but she'd never look lovely, or a sharp, snappy dresser like me or my husband. We had that in common, like our love for the house.

'Your husband's a looker,' said Bridget then. It was almost as if she'd read my mind. I nodded, went on.

'Gareth loves clothes like he loves the house, and you know how much he cares about that. He used to drive past on his way to work, and wonder how he'd ever afford it, that's why he works so hard, even now. He really wanted to own that house. I hope you don't mind.'

'And now he does,' said Bridget, smiling. 'And of course I don't mind, somebody had to, I'm glad it was you.'

*But was she really?* I wondered, thinking. The home she had now, if far from a slum, was so much more... ordinary, so suburban.

'Your David must be quite successful,' I said to Bridget, wanting to please her, make her feel liked.

'Well, yes, that's quite true, but he's older now, and our children are too, they've lives of their own, they've flown the nest. We no longer need such a huge possession. Although, we didn't *have* to sell it.' She paused, thinking.

'Samantha and David never had kids, so after they split, she said she'd leave, she told him once she'd hated the house. He gave her a settlement, some sort of payoff, although he told me she didn't deserve one. He was glad to be rid of her, in the end. So, then, when we married, the sensible thing was for me to move in. I thought I didn't mind, I was glad to be with him, I thought the house was what I wanted.' Bridget went on.

'I tried not to mention Samantha, you know. He never seemed to get over it all.' She leant across me and reached in her bag. 'Here, that's them on the day they got married. David doesn't know I've got this photo.' She handed me a faded old print. I glanced at the picture, the colours were weird, had changed over time. They were all blues and reds.

'That's David,' she said, nodding at the photo and pointing at her husband. 'And there, beside him, that's Samantha, she didn't wear white, even on her wedding day, wasn't that odd, way back then? She looks quite glamorous, don't you think? Unlike the tart she eventually became.' Bridget sniffed.

I stared at the photo, feeling cold, there was something about seeing the couple together, knowing she was dead, and not just dead, but dead as in *murdered*, by persons unknown. David's hand was on hers in the photo, they were cutting the cake, the knife they were holding seemed so out of place. *Start as you mean to go on, David.* Why would Bridget keep such a thing?

'He no longer has that suit,' said Bridget. 'I made him throw out all of those things, the things from *before*.'

From when he was married to *her*, she meant.

'*They're* rather nice,' I said to Bridget, talking about her husband's cufflinks, more for something to say than anything. They were shaped like trains and quite distinctive. I didn't much like them, if I was honest, but I knew they couldn't have been bought in a chain store. Bridget just smiled.

'He's always loved trains,' she told me, amused, 'he's even got track set up in the attic. But, these, yes, they were rather special, quite expensive, or so I was told. He thinks she took them when she left. I can't say I'm sorry, as it happens, it saved me having to throw them out.'

Because they were part of his life with her. She didn't have to say it.

'Of course he couldn't prove she'd taken them,' Bridget went on, 'like the affair, it was just speculation. But they *were* designer, they would have been valuable, unlike her dress. I didn't even know that was in your attic.'

Silence fell on our little table, today, for once, we were feeling sombre, Samantha's photo had touched a few nerves. Love and loss and death, intermingling. I wanted to get out, and into the sunshine. Bridget coughed.

'Enough about that dreadful woman, tell me about your delectable husband. Does he spoil you, like David spoils me?'

'Oh, yes,' I told her, eager to boast, I wanted to prove my husband was the best. 'You know I told you he wanted your house? Well, Gareth's a man of decisive mind. When he first saw me, he said to himself, *I have to have her,* and not just for bed, but for something serious, more committed. He's always buying me lovely gifts.'

'I'm sure he is,' said Bridget, smiling. If only she knew.

I thought of all the building work, the way I always had to be smart, the car he'd bought after seeing our neighbour's, the hallmark of a successful man. Proving himself and not just to me. I smiled, proudly. 'I've got to go,' I said to Bridget, I couldn't help feeling sorry for the woman. Yes, she was loved, but her life was over, luxurious, true, but on the decline, settled, decided, whereas ours was, what? I wasn't quite sure, but on the up, I was sure about that.

I thought about what I'd be wearing for dinner, for a special dinner in honour of my husband, he'd won some award, for sales or something. For being the best in the area team. I wasn't surprised.

When I got back, I stared at my dress, it had never been worn, the shop had only delivered it that morning. It had already been pressed, it didn't even need an iron running over it. But it needed something, that necklace I'd had for my twenty-first birthday, a platinum chain with a heart-shaped diamond. That would do. I couldn't find it.

I searched all over the house for that necklace, I had to have it, I knew the dress would be wrong without it. I even emptied the kitchen cupboards, although I knew it wouldn't be there. I wondered if the builders had taken it. *No*, I thought, that's paranoid thinking.

Gareth would never forgive me, I knew, if I wasn't looking my absolute best. So I kept on looking, as time ticked on. But still no necklace.

Just before six, my husband came home, smiling, triumphant and ready to play his part like a king. He wandered into our walk-in wardrobe, a room really, I hardly ever used it, I thought a room just for clothes was indulgent, it was where I'd been looking for my jewellery. I should have been happy, I'd just found it, in a very old suitcase belonging to Gareth, along with a watch I'd lost recently.

And a pair of cufflinks, shaped like trains.

© Ellie Stevenson 2015

# About the Authors

**Nick Sproxton** is an artist and writer who produces mainly short stories and some poetry. He is currently working on a novel for a young adult readership which explores in an imaginative way problems of identity, relationships and our fragmentary understanding of reality. These themes provide the focus for all his written work in which the fragility and insecurity of our lives is examined.

**Sharon Hopwood** is a children's writer and creator of children's animation concepts. A member of the SCBWI, Sharon is a lively and popular storyteller at nurseries, schools and literary events. Sharon is currently working on her latest series of stories for 8-12 year olds, *The Mappleford Mysteries*. 'The Halloween Mask' is a short story based on characters from *The Mappleford Mysteries*. Find out more about Sharon at:
**www.hopwoodtoons.com**
**http://twitter.com/Hopwoodtoons**

**Pam Pattison:** Pam couldn't remember a time when she didn't want to write, but publication didn't come until she was in her thirties and had some success with short stories in women's magazines.

Now a pensioner, she has recently completed courses in creative writing with the Open University and was encouraged to widen her horizons and experiment with other genres including poetry and a short stage play.

Currently, she is about halfway through an historical novel and admits to being easily distracted, and is toying with an idea for a children's story. So much to write: so little time.

**Elizabeth Cox** has enjoyed a life-long passion for literature and this has fostered her desire to write both fiction and poetry.

As a mature student she returned to study literature at the University of Warwick, gaining an MA in Gender, Literature, and Modernity followed by a PhD in nineteenth-century Gothic literature by British women writers.

She is currently working on a novella, set in the nineteenth century, which draws upon the concepts (such as representations of gender, sexual identity and sexual desire) that she examined in her PhD.

**Tim Binder:** in the past Tim has written articles for various publications, and recently co-authored a book (*Walk with the Wise*): a series of reflections on quotations from poetry and prose.

Retirement has now given him the leisure and opportunity to realise a long held dream – writing a book reflecting on literature and art, as seen through his experiences of life and nature.

**Bren Littlewood**, writing under the pen name of JJ Franklin, has written scripts for the BBC. Her first novel, *Urge to Kill,* is a psychological thriller featuring DI Matt Turrell. The book is set in and around Stratford-upon-Avon.

The second book in the series, *Echoes of Justice*, will be published in 2015. She is a member of The Writers' Guild, The Alliance of Independent Authors and Equity.

Buy *Urge to Kill* at Waterstones or on Amazon: **www.amazon.co.uk/Urge-Kill-1-JJ-Franklin-ebook/dp/B008K7Y47K**

**Beryl Downing** is the author of two Penguin non-fiction books and a recently published anthology of wacky research projects called *They Must Be Joking*. As a feature writer for *The Times* and contributor to national magazines, she is more used to writing 1000 words at a time than full-length fiction, but has just completed the first section of a five-part novel. Find her website at

**www.berylouisedowning.co.uk**

**Jeff Brades** is currently close to completion on the first in a six book series depicting a working career spanning 30 countries in five continents, including Russia, China, India and the United States. Looking to self-publish the series, Jeff values time spent with the group to learn and understand how best to do this. Previously, Jeff has had short stories, and sporting journalism articles published, but is now concentrating on this series as the primary output.

**Kathy McMaster** has become involved with creative writing courses and writing groups over the last two years. One of her lifetime ambitions is to publish a novel.

To this end she has been improving her writing skills and gaining knowledge on how to approach agents and self-publish, as well as working on her novel. She also writes short stories, mostly for competitions.

**Jann Tracy:** since retiring she has become an enthusiastic volunteer for a variety of organisations, and is working on a number of non-fiction titles intended for the ebook market.

**Jennie Dobson** is a freelance writer of articles, short stories and novels. At 15 she became the youngest press officer in the country and honed her writing skills on daily press releases about ice cream and budgerigars. She went on to research historical novels for established authors and became an editor, proof-reader and copy editor for various publishing houses. She is currently writing an historical novel but continues to get articles published on subjects as diverse as pauper apprentices, flying and Shakespeare. **www.jenniedobsonwriter.com**

**Ingrid Stevens:** word-besotted writer, blogger and translator, eternally at odds with time choices. Poems and articles published in *Pierrot, Die Zeit, Rheinische Post, Stratford Herald* and lots online.

Her prose (young adults' journeying and science fiction) is still drawer-ridden. Find her at **http://lingoservice.wordpress.com**

**Jacci Gooding** is an author and book-reviewer of independent and e-published books, based in the West Midlands. She has had several items published in traditional magazine format as well as online, and has won writing competitions.

At the time of going to press, Jacci has completed her first novel and is preparing it for publication. Find her on Twitter **@JacciGooding** or at **www.jaccigoodingauthor.com** Jacci is also a member of the Bardstown Writers and the Alliance of Independent Authors.

**Marilyn Rodwell** has had a varied career, as a teacher, nurse, business owner, and lecturer in Business. For the last few years she has been writing fiction, mainly historical fiction set between 1917 and 1930, post the Indentureship of Indian labour in the Caribbean.

The first of the trilogy is *The Last Year of Childhood,* set in a small village in Trinidad, where 12 year old Latchmin is struggling to escape an arranged marriage, in order to become a teacher.

**Dianne Lee** was born in Leamington Spa and educated at the local girls' college. Just prior to retirement, she began writing children's sci-fi adventure novels and poetry.

Since joining the Bardstown Writers' Group, Dianne has also written some short stories.

**David Nelmes:** a blind writer, David gave up his day job to be apprenticed to WG Stanton, a renowned BBC dramatist. This resulted in a number of short story publications, an award for his use of dialogue, an agent (now bankrupt) and the freedom to follow Dickens's advice ('once having set out my characters to play out the play, then it is their job to do it, as it were, and not mine') to guide him in the production of two novels, one first drafted and laid to grow cold, the other currently being produced in final draft.

**Ellie Stevenson** has written two novels, *Shadows of the Lost Child* (Rosegate Publications, 2014; Amazon: B00NGSSVM2) and *Ship of Haunts: the other Titanic story* (Rosegate Publications, 2012; Amazon: B007SPGR98), both partly historical mysteries with a dash of the mystical and some ghosts. *Shadows* was inspired by historic York (UK).

Ellie has also written *Watching Charlotte Brontë Die: and other surreal stories* (Rosegate Publications, 2013; Amazon: B00AZYXASU). Her writing is fuelled by inspiration, determination and plenty of coffee. Find her at
**www.facebook.com/Stevensonauthor** or
**http://elliestevenson.wordpress.com**

# Acknowledgements

Bardstown Writers would like to thank everyone who contributed to the production of our second anthology. Special thanks must go to Colin Flint of Stratford-upon-Avon College and the students who entered the cover design and logo competition last year. Congratulations to this year's winner, Grace Kemp (cover design) and also to Elliott Parkes who designed the Bardstown Writers' logo.